TO BED WITH GRAND MUSIC

Persephone Book N° 86
Published by Persephone Books Ltd 2009

First published in 1946 by
Pilot Press Ltd by 'Sarah Russell'

© The Estate of Marghanita Laski

Preface © Juliet Gardiner 2009

Endpapers taken from a Jacqmar scarf
'Good Night Everybody' c. 1940,
in a private collection

Typeset in ITC Baskerville by
Keystroke, Tettenhall, Wolverhampton

Printed and bound in Germany by
GGP Media GmbH, Poessneck

9781903155769

Persephone Books Ltd
59 Lamb's Conduit Street
London WC1N 3NB
020 7242 9292

www.persephonebooks.co.uk

TO BED WITH GRAND MUSIC

by

'SARAH RUSSELL'

(MARGHANITA LASKI)

with a new preface by

JULIET GARDINER

PERSEPHONE BOOKS

LONDON

PREFACE

To Bed with Grand Music is the story of a female rake's progress in wartime Britain. Deborah Robertson, a young and pretty wife and mother, definitely does *not* keep the home fires burning while her husband is away at war. The novel opens quite brilliantly with Deborah and her husband Graham in bed together at the end of his embarkation leave. The next morning he is to set off on active service – or rather a desk job in Cairo – leaving Deborah and their toddler son Timmy at home in Hampshire. The couple are talking about fidelity.

> 'Listen, darling,' [Graham says] 'I'm not going to promise you I'll be physically faithful to you, because I don't want to make you any promise I may not be able to keep. God alone knows how long I may be stuck in Mid-East, and it's no good saying I can do without a woman for three or four years, because I can't. But I'll promise you this, I'll never let myself fall in love with anyone else, and I'll never sleep with anyone who could possibly fill your place in any part of my life.' He

was himself a little overawed with the magnanimity of his proposal. That means I'll have to be pretty damn careful, he said to himself, but aloud he said, 'Darling, will you promise me the same?'

Deborah, of course, does, fervently, swearing that her love for Graham will 'prevent her doing anything about it' no matter how much she might be attracted to any other man. But Graham is not prepared to improve on his offer. And so the couple attempt to navigate the emotional peaks, inevitable at such a fraught moment, succeed and part, each swearing undying adoration for the other.

The story of Deborah's fall from grace fills the rest of the book. What happens to Graham is less clear, but whatever adventures he has in the gay social whirl that was Cairo in wartime (so well evoked in Artemis Cooper's 1989 *Cairo in the War* as a place that meant 'fleshpots or brass hats' to the troops, and 'polo and opulent parties' to the officers), he clearly sticks to his commitment not to let anyone replace his wife in his affections, regardless of who might, or might not, be in his bed.

At first Deborah is content in her not particularly demanding life as a young mother since she has help in the form of her loyal housekeeper, Mrs Chalmers. There are bridge parties, shopping trips, the usual round of a young middle-class wife in the 1940s, war or not, but soon she begins to get 'nervy', and irritable with her child. Her redoubtable mother, Mrs Betts, the sagacious widow of a Leeds merchant and town councillor, decides, in cahoots with Mrs Chalmers,

that what Deborah needs is a job to 'take her out of herself'. But rather than opting for interesting-sounding work in nearby Winchester that would allow her plenty of time at home, Deborah decides to go to London to share a flat with Madeleine, a worldly-wise friend from her days as an art student at the Slade, and only to return home to her two-year-old at weekends.

Soon, all too predictably, rather than staying in in the evening eating a tin of baked beans, reading the evening paper from cover to cover and conscientiously missing her husband, Deborah, almost accidently, embarks on a series of affairs, each with a progressively rather less upright character than the one before. Hers is now a world of smart restaurants, cocktail bars, nightclubs, little black dresses, frivolous concoctions of hats, jewels and black market perfume – it is all rather reminiscent of the world evoked in some of Mollie Panter-Downes' short stories *Good Evening, Mrs Craven* (Persephone Book No. 8), particularly in the eponymous story. '"The War Office doesn't have a service for sending telegrams to mistresses, does it?"' asks 'Mrs Craven' bleakly. Or an even closer fit with the real life war of the *femme fatale* Barbara Skelton, a self-confessed 'night flitter' around London before she got a job in Cairo in 1942 through the good agency of Donald Maclean, working as a Foreign Office 'cipherine' and having an affair with King Farouk. Before she was posted abroad, Skelton had met a French banker, Boris, who 'had been the Chef de Cabinet du Ministère des Finances under Léon Blum' and came to London with General de Gaulle after the fall of France.

Separated from his wife in Paris . . . Monsieur Boris was
desperate for a woman and I seemed to fit the bill . . .
As though to seek oblivion, we led a hectic social life.
Pre-luncheon drinks in the Curzon Street Sherry Bar,
luncheons at the Ritz, the Coquille, the Ecu de France
or the Coq d'Or in Mayfair. When we were not at the
400, we frequented a vast vulgar nightclub off Berkeley
Square; the Conga had a revolving dance floor. Or
one went to the Suivi or the Jamboree and, of course
there was always the Players' Theatre Club . . .' (*Tears
Before Bedtime* 1987).

It is this same brittle, febrile, pleasure-seeking wartime
world of heightened emotions and brief sexual encounters
that Laski evokes through Deborah, a mother neglectful of
her child, a wife who suggests selling her husband's grandmother's pearls, intended to be 'handed down to Timmy's
wife in the dim and distant future', to clear the debts she
has incurred keeping up an extravagant lifestyle. The fasci-
nation of *To Bed with Grand Music* is its unusual recreation
of one aspect of the Home Front in the Second World War.
It is an exaggerated, near harlot's tale without doubt, but it
has a wry authenticity and provides a refreshing counterpoint
to all the usual wartime novels of sterling women making
do and mending, managing on reduced money since their
husbands are receiving army pay, putting in long hours in
munitions factories or with the WVS, eking out rations,
going without themselves, spending hour queuing for a 'bit of
fish' or a few slices of offal, getting through their evenings

writing to their soldier or sailor or airman husband, boyfriend or son, and dreaming of nothing but his return. Deborah Robertson is about as far as it is possible to get from Jocelyn Playfair's heroine Cressida Chance in *A House in the Country* (Persephone Book No. 31), 'a born comforter' holding it all together with her 'cabbages in neat rows, and a pie in the oven . . . allowing people to stay in her house because the war has filled the country with people with nowhere to live.' Being stalwart and scrubbing her deal kitchen table 'till it was as white as cloth' and feeding her 'guests' nourishing meals, Cressida triumphantly passes the 'test of war' by staying put and keeping calm and carrying on and trying not to worry, and cheering everyone up round the Aga.

Marghanita Laski's book's appeal lies in its portrayal of someone who signally failed the 'test of war', and in its evocation of a fractured and transient society during the exigencies and contingencies of wartime: Deborah's lovers are married, most have children, all are in London only briefly, as were so many from overseas – allies and exiles from occupied countries – during the Second World War. All regard their affairs – as Deborah herself initially does – as a by-product of the extraordinary circumstances of war. They have no relevance to, and will not be allowed to intrude on, their normal peacetime lives – and marriages. They are as ships that pass, connect, and pass on in the night of wartime, when the motto is so often live for today for tomorrow you may die.

However, although *To Bed with Grand Music* chronicles an immorality that is all the more shocking since the

bed-hopping and high-living frivolity is enacted against a backdrop of sacrifice and danger, of trust and commitment, at a time when those made a much proselytised contribution to morale, it is not itself an immoral book, although it is a cautionary one. Marghanita Laski writes with compassion about human frailties and foibles and is at her best when she is writing about self-deception – a trick she pulled off with almost equal aplomb in her first novel of wartime, *Love on the Supertax* (1944), which is a parody of a 1930s bestseller, Walter Greenwood's *Love on the Dole*. Deborah's arguments with herself – usually, it has to be said, very easily settled – about whether what she is doing is wrong, are delightful vignettes of cant and delusion. It is only fair to Timmy that she should not be edgy, therefore it is in his interest that she should sleep with her escorts (an argument she angrily rejects when her American lover, Joe, first advances it, but which she soon wholeheartedly embraces); it is patriotic for women to do their bit in wartime – albeit by working in an antique shop selling *faux* historic trinkets to visiting US GIs; it would be unfair to Mrs Chalmers to return home and deprive her of Timmy's company, etc.

Yet *To Bed with Grand Music* is not a tragic book – Graham's posting does not put him in the firing line, the bombs miss Timmy on the one occasion he does come up to town (although, despite her best intentions, Deborah does not go to him during an air raid, but is persuaded by her latest escort to stay in the restaurant and finish her meal) – but it is a book with an undertow of sadness, a wistful book, perhaps a tragi-comedy. What will happen in the future to the pettish,

avaricious minx Deborah has become? '"There's no going back", Deborah's mind said to her . . . "there's no going back . . . no profit in examining motives, in totting up gain, nothing but going forward to gaiety and loss and loss."' When peace meant austerity and there were no longer handsome men with plenty of money out for a good time, who will play court to her? How will she remake a life with Graham and Timmy in their little cottage in the country after the glamour and thrills of a cosmopolitan wartime capital?

These were real questions to ask at the end of the war. Peace was what everyone wanted: the troops home, life going on just as before. But it wasn't like that: it couldn't be. Many men had been away for years, some of course had terrible, harrowing experiences, and coming back to the old routines was very hard. Wartime life was regimented, regulated and ordered: now families had to relearn how to live a normal life with all its many stresses and strains, and some found it all but impossible. Many men missed the easy 'buddydom' of the forces and regretted that the authority they had enjoyed seemed to evaporate as soon as they returned home. Women, who thought that all they had wanted in the world was to have their man back home again, found they had had to grow independent and self reliant in his absence and that it was tough to readjust to deferring to – or at least consulting – a husband. Many children hardly knew their father – nor he them – and resented the presence of a stranger in the house, in Mummy's bed. It was one thing to say 'Don't you know there's a war on?' to excuse shortages and difficulties, but now after years of food and clothes rationing, fuel shortages and

travel limitations, there was the dreary prospect of wartime conditions stretching on for many years, with little to brighten or ease lives, and few goods in the shops, since most of Britain's manufacturing output was going for exports to pay for the country's war debts.

The dislocations and disruptions of war put many marriages under strain. Numerous people, caught up in the drama, had married hastily – and young. There was a certain poignant glamour to an absent, brave, fighting husband, but after so long a separation, it was sometimes hard to remember what the attraction had been all that time ago. 'It's a funny position, to be married and yet not married; you can't go out with the fellows, and so you're alone all the time'; 'War wives are like a single girl'; 'six years married and away in the army for five' were typical comments (Juliet Gardiner *Wartime*).

Many men undoubtedly had affairs abroad, and some women left at home did so too – 'drifting' in the terminology of the times into another man's arms. A medical officer who served with the army in the Middle East during the war reckoned that two years separation was about as much as a marriage could stand: 'after the third and subsequent years an increasing proportion of wives lapsed', he concluded. After that commitment became elastic, memories dimmed and couples started to drift apart (*Wartime*). '"I'm a normal healthy woman",' Deborah tells Graham's friend Ken, who calls on her, '"and the years without – well, without anything, haven't been easy. I don't expect you to understand that," she added. "It's not a thing men are expected to endure."'

'Affairs in wartime were almost inevitable', recalled a married former nurse Ethel Mattison, who had one herself. The advice columns of wartime magazines condemned women who had affairs while their men were away fighting, but were even more waspish about the luxury of confession, insisting that it was *not* helpful to a man's morale to write to tell him about misdemeanours. 'Every married man out here is haunted in one way and another with the idea of the crack-up of his marriage: some poor chaps dread the very sound of American or Canadian troops' wrote a British serviceman stationed in Palestine to his wife (*Wartime*).

Women were often prepared to forgive wartime infidelities as transient and exceptional, and some men could too, but many found it harder to forget – particularly if there was concrete evidence in the shape of an illegitimate child. The figure of 300,000 illegitimate babies born during the war years, double the number born in the same pre-war period, does not, of course, include those born to married women but not fathered by her husband. However, this steep rise does not necessarily indicate looser morals: in pre-war Britain most women probably only slept with the man they were intending to marry, so if they became pregnant, this simply advanced the wedding; 70 per cent of out of wedlock conceptions were reckoned to be regularised in this way, but in wartime with men often posted away at short notice, this avenue was not always open.

In the 1930s the most common form of contraception had been the age-old method of coitus interruptus, however to be effective this requires trust and a stable relationship,

and many wartime romances were far from that, being fleeting encounters, an intense response to extraordinary times. Latex for condoms was in short supply after the fall of Malaya and what was available was prioritised for the teats of babies' feeding bottles and other necessities. But since Deborah Robertson seemed somehow to be able to wheedle most of what she wanted, perhaps avoiding providing a little brother or sister for Timmy did not prove too much of a problem for her or her string of lovers. Moreover, while abortion on non medical grounds was illegal, that did not mean it did not happen either in expensive if somewhat shady clinics for women like Deborah, or with back street abortionists, or self induced using castor oil, penny royal, or quinine and hot baths or jumping down stairs for poorer women. In 1939, a report estimated that almost 20 per cent of pregnancies ended in abortion – up to 150,000 a year – and a quarter of these were probably criminal. And undoubtedly this figure rose during the war. Further evidence of the stress of war on marriage was the steep rise in the number of divorces, peaking at 47,041 in 1947, the year after *To Bed with Grand Music* was published. And for the first time more husbands petitioned for divorce than wives – surely a significant wartime shift in behaviour and expectations.

Nevertheless, *To Bed with Grand Music* is a book very much against the grain – it was, after all, published in 1946 just a year after the end of the war, when emotions were still raw, and no doubt there was still a lot of hypocrisy and pretence before the hairline cracks began to appear and it became possible to acknowledge openly that life had not

entirely been a matter of linking arms and singing 'There'll Always Be an England' as a nation of crypto-cheery Cockneys scrambled from the ruins of the old world, that there had been another story, of getting round regulations, bending the rules, of profiting from war, of deceit, irresponsibility and having a good time while others sacrificed and suffered.

Marghanita Laski's novel is an ahead-of-the-pack telling of an aspect of the civilian's war it was not yet acceptable to reveal, exposing aspects of its darker side, its other wounds. Perhaps that was an important reason why, on the whole, it was not well received at the time. Michael Sadler, writing in the *Sunday Times*, described it as 'a novel of wartime decadence'; Howard Spring in his weekly column 'What I've Been Reading' in the *Sunday Graphic* referred to it as 'A most unpleasant novel . . . fearsome and tragic'; while Glyn Gordon, reviewing the book for the *Sunday Pictorial*, sneered 'there is nothing "Grand" about Miss Russell's flamboyant tale of music and wartime unfaithfulness'. He then went on to reveal the post-war unease he and so many others clearly felt, claiming that this 'sensational' novel 'has no place in the homes of the nation striving to regain the precious normality war took away . . .' But a fellow novelist, Olivia Manning, whose opinion Marghanita Laski no doubt would have valued, was both more perceptive and more honest. Reviewing *To Bed with Grand Music* for the *Palestine Post* she described the book as 'very well told without sentiment, and with sufficient irony to give it an air of wit'. Having spent much of her war in Cairo, and written her trilogy *Fortunes of War* about that time, Manning (who also sometimes wrote under a pseudonym, Jacob Morrow) reflected that she had observed such behaviour among soldiers posted abroad, and was interested to see how those left behind on the Home Front dealt with such temptations.

As Jenny Hartley reminds us in *Millions Like Us: British Women's Fiction in the Second World War*, 'novels about women who contemplate and reject the idea of having affairs proliferated towards the end of the war', and she instances Elizabeth Taylor's *At Mrs Lippincote's*, Betty Miller's *On the Side of the Angels* and Winfred Peck's *There is a Fortress*, all published in 1945.

But Marghanita Laski's novel pushed harder: Deborah Robertson, pretty much a tart without a heart by mid-way through the book, exemplifies war's dark underside, its heightened passions – the undoubted eroticism of danger – its moral fragility and pervasive aura of contumely and temptations succumbed to. It is a portrait we have perhaps come to understand better now through reading such novels as Elizabeth Bowen's *The Heat of the Day*, and more recently Sarah Waters' *The Night Watch*, and watching episodes of *Foyle's War*.

The Second World War offered unique temptations; the obverse of every noble deed was the possibility of a traitorous betrayal. Rationing, both of food and clothes and of petrol, spawned a thriving black market, under the counter practices trading necessities and hard to obtain luxuries such as silk stockings, perfume, cosmetics, drink. And rationing, which promised fair shares for all, wasn't always fair at all: fruit was never rationed but a single peach could cost 7/6d,

a bunch of grapes 25 shillings, when an Army private's pay was around £3 a week. Bon viveurs such as 'Chips' Channon and Harold Nicolson still managed to drink several magnums of champagne at the Dorchester in 1940. Grand restaurants of the sort Deborah Robertson came to frequent got round the ban on charging more than five shillings for a meal by such devices as adding an exorbitant cover charge, or fabulously overcharging for wine. And when that principled Bloomsbury pacifist, Frances Partridge, and her husband entertained friends to lunch at their Wiltshire home in May 1941, somehow lampreys, *foie gras* and champagne were on the menu (cf. *A Pacifist's War* 1978), while most housewives were wondering how on earth they could make the cheese ration of around 4 ounces per person per week stretch a little further.

The black-out and the blitz provided cover for criminal acts – handbags snatched, wallets lifted in darkened streets, bombed houses looted even before the ARP services arrived, servicemen AWOL, conning their way without the necessary identification that wartime regulations required, even an occasional murder committed in the hope that the body would be thought to have been that of an air raid victim. And then there was sex.

In 1939 the Ministry of Health alerted local authorities: 'It is well known that a statement of war favours the spread of VD in the population' and put this down to 'lack of self control' and the 'excitement of war'. The Ministry was proved right: by 1941 the incidence of venereal diseases had increased by 70 per cent since the start of the war, and in

London and ports such as Liverpool, Cardiff and Glasgow, the rise was even steeper (cf. John Costello *Love, Sex and War* 1985). It almost reached epidemic proportions with the arrival of the first US troops in Britain in 1942, rising to nearly sixty cases per thousand GIs stationed in the UK by 1943.

When the authorities – American and British – held a conference in March 1943 to discuss this moral laxity, they concluded that the black-out had a lot to do with it, as did the presence of forces from overseas with plenty of money, too much time, and without the stabilising influence of family and friends, as well as young girls 'anxious to have a good time' after a hard day in the munitions factory. So, as well as the increase in prostitution, 'ladies of the night' sidling up to servicemen offering 'a good time, soldier' in exchange for money, there were the 'Piccadilly Commandoes' and 'Hyde Park rangers' propositioning soldiers on leave in London, the opportunism of the 'goodtime girls' or 'amateur whores'. A whole spectrum: women on the make, prepared to sleep with a man – or go up an alleyway or into a shop doorway with him – in return for money, to those who proved to be of 'easy virtue' if nylon stockings, perfume, a good time, was on offer. Deborah Robertson would have hardly thought of herself as being on such a spectrum, but that was where she was albeit at the discreet, sophisticated end.

Little wonder then, that the waters closed as the war ended: anxieties that society might have lost its moral compass, that family life could have been irreparably damaged, made reviewers jumpy and condemnatory at the picture *To Bed with Grand Music* painted.

Marghanita Laski, who was born into a distinguished family of Jewish intellectuals and was educated at St Paul's Girls School, which she disliked, and Somerville College, Oxford, was a committed atheist, who nevertheless pondered deeply and wrote and argued extensively about spirituality – including from pulpits all over London. She was remarkably well read with a catholic taste in literature – she was such a fast reader that she claimed to read as many as ten crime novels a day – had strongly held opinions, eloquently voiced in a way that did not easily brook argument, a questioning mind, and an autocratic and a frequently intimidating manner. She is probably best remembered today as a broadcaster: she frequently took part in *The Brains Trust* and *Any Questions* and became a regular on *The Critics* and its successor *Critics Forum* as well as the less well remembered *Everybody's Songs*. She reviewed books for *The Observer* and *The Listener* and numerous other publications, largely so that she would always have something to read, was an insistent firer-off of letters to the press on numerous subjects, a rigorous Vice-Chairman of the Arts Council, and served to great purpose on Lord [Noel] Annan's Committee on the Future of Broadcasting from 1974 to 1977.

But it was the English language that was her real love. If Miss Laski was unimpressed with someone she was wont to describe them as 'under-dictionaried'. She, on the other hand, was profoundly 'over-dictionaried', and put this to most effective use when she responded to a request from her friend Dr Robert Burchfield for illustrative quotations for the four supplements to the Oxford English Dictionary that

he was editing. By the time the fourth volume was published in 1986 Laski had sent in about a quarter of a million quotations – far more than any other contributor – including five examples of the use of the word 'bathmat' – and had reread the entire works of Dickens, Charlotte M Yonge, George Eliot, Mrs Gaskell and many other nineteenth century novelists – and much more besides, including Edwardian sales catalogues and almost every thriller ever published – to provide examples. In 1963 Mayflower Books published an unexpurgated version of John Cleland's 1748 bawdy comic novel *Memoirs of a Woman of Pleasure*, commonly known as *Fanny Hill*, and was promptly prosecuted under the Obscenity Act. Marghanita Laski spoke for the defence, claiming that the book was important since it illustrated the first use in English literature of certain words. When asked by the judge to give an example, she paused, and then volunteered crisply 'chaise-longue'.

So, why did this forceful and confident woman decide to write under the pseudonym of 'Sarah Russell', one she sometimes used when reviewing crime fiction? Embarrassment 'is an unlikely motive for camouflage in the twentieth century,' suggests the literary scholar, John Mullan, who argues that the author figure has become increasingly important in the marketing of books and when anonymity or pseudonymity is present in modern novels, another explanation must be sought (*Anonymity* 2007). But *To Bed with Grand Music* was not Laski's first book, nor was it so unlike her other novels – it is very similar in style to *Love on the Supertax* – that she might wish to make a distinction between the two and create a subgenre of her work – like Ruth Rendell writing as

'Barbara Vine', for example, or Julian Barnes becoming 'Dan Kavanagh' (or even Iain Banks writing as Iain M Banks). It is not a book with a pointed political message – unlike, say, *The Village*, an indictment of the class system – which Laski may have thought would have more purchase if it were not apparent that she was the author. *To Bed with Grand Music* by Sarah Russell was published by the Pilot Press for which John Howard, Marghanita Laski's husband, had worked, a press better known for its glossy wartime books on subjects such as post-war reconstruction written by such weighty figures as Sir William Beveridge, the poet and one of the founders of Mass-Observation, Charles Madge, and Julian Huxley. But it was not the subject matter that made its publication a surprise, but the fact that it was only after the war that the Pilot Press – which did not long survive - started to publish novels at all.

Was it autobiographical? Reader, consider the summary of Marghanita Laski's life and character outlined above! In fact she spent the early years of the war largely with her children and their grandmother in North Oxford, later moving to Abbots Langley in Hertfordshire (the village of her eponymously named novel).

Yet the itch, perversely, remained: in the complaint of the cultural critic Ronald Barthes, 'the *explanation* of the work is still sought in the person of its producer' ('The Death of the Author' 1986). That shortcut seemed, frustratingly, denied. The answer finally came from Laski's daughter, Lydia Howard. 'Deborah Robertson is based on someone my mother knew. She was fascinated and upset at seeing what

the war had done to this person, and decided to write about it in a novel. She did not write under her own name in case the woman realised that she was the anti-heroine of the book, or that someone might be able to identify her as an acquaintance of my mother's.' Moreover, the real life Deborah Robertson did not have a seedy post-war existence. She never did pick up the pieces of her married life with 'Graham': the two were divorced and 'Deborah' made a successful second marriage to a wealthy man, and no doubt lived the sort of life her fictional *doppelganger* would have much envied.

Juliet Gardiner
London, 2009

TO BED WITH GRAND MUSIC

CHAPTER ONE

❦❧❦❧❦

Graham and Deborah Robertson lay in bed together and tried to say goodbye to each other.

Deborah whimpered, 'I can't let you go, I can't,' and then lay shivering with the uselessness of her protest.

Graham moved away from her a little, and sighed. 'Darling,' he said, 'darling, don't make it harder for me. God alone knows the last thing on earth I want is to go away from you, but there's just damn all I can do about it. Darling, don't you think I shan't be missing you every hour of every day, thinking how bloody attractive you are and that I'm not here to be with you?'

Deborah flung herself upon him, digging her nails into his neck. She sobbed, 'You're a swine to say such things, you know I love you and I'll always love you. Darling, my darling, you don't have to worry about me, promise you'll never worry about me in that way, because I swear you don't have to.' She paused and stopped crying. With an ugly edge to her voice, she said, 'Anyway, what about you?'

There was a moment's silence, then Graham pushed his arm under her shoulders and held her close to him.

'Listen darling,' he said, 'I'm not going to promise you I'll be physically faithful to you, because I don't want to make you any promise I may not be able to keep. God alone knows how long I may be stuck in Mid-East, and it's no good saying I can do without a woman for three or four years, because I can't. But I'll promise you this, I'll never let myself fall in love with anyone else, and I'll never sleep with anyone who could possibly fill your place in any part of my life.' He was himself a little overawed with the magnanimity of his proposal. That means I'll have to be pretty damn careful, he said to himself, but aloud he said, 'Darling, will you promise me the same?'

Deborah, who had lain quietly in the familiar reassurance of her husband's arm, now sat up in bed, taut with emotion, and said stiffly, 'I promise you I will always be faithful to you, however long you're away. I love you, and even if I wanted another man, my love for you would prevent me doing any-thing about it.' She stopped and wondered frantically, isn't that enough to make him say the same, if I can do it, he can. But he remained silent, and she drooped a little, then added, 'Besides, I've got Timmy.'

Both fell with relief on this theme which seemed to offer a momentary relief from tension and the possibility of com-plete agreement. Graham said, 'You'll see he doesn't forget me, won't you, darling?'

'He can't possibly forget you,' said Deborah firmly, 'I'll be talking about you most of the time to him – after all you're the main thing we've got in common. It seems to me the danger is much more that he'll come to idealise you too

much, and have such a splendid picture of you in his mind, that you won't be able to live up to it when you *do* come back to us.'

'He's a nice baby,' Graham said, thinking wholly of his two-year-old son, of his soft fair hair, his smooth skin, his sudden chuckles, the pleased recognition in his eyes. 'Deborah, you're glad we had him, aren't you?'

The atmosphere of the imminent parting settled down on them again. Deborah said, 'I think I'd go mad if I hadn't got him. But with Timmy and our home, I've got something solid to stick to. I mean, whatever I do for Timmy or for the cottage, I'm doing, in a way, for you, and for our life together afterwards. It's all a part of you and me.'

They lay clasped together in the darkness, then Deborah said with a spurt of bitterness, 'But if I hadn't got him, I'd move heaven and earth to get a job in Cairo and be with you. Some people leave their babies and do that anyway, and then they have their second one out there. Probably Timmy will be much too old before we can have another now.'

Graham felt a deep weariness at this farewell. Each emotional peak surmounted revealed only a higher one beyond. But he said patiently, 'Darling, the last thing on earth I'd let you do would be to come to Cairo now. It looks as if Rommel will be there before I am, anyway, and David's last airgraph said that practically all the women and children were being sent out.'

'Well,' said Deborah angrily, 'I don't want you to leave me in order to languish in a German prison camp for the rest of the war.'

'Look here,' Graham said, in equal anger, 'don't you think it would be better if we both forgot for a moment about all the bloody things that might happen and look on what you could call the bright side? Parting from you is unutterable hell, but really we're damn lucky. I'm going out to a staff job that's as safe as anything reasonably can be. You're staying here in our own home with our own baby to look after. I love and adore you and always shall, I shall never be unfaithful to you in any way that even you could possibly mind, and we know that as soon as the war is over we're going to be together again and have everything we had before, only better.' He paused. Beside him, Deborah was sobbing quietly, but now there was no anger in her sobs. He picked up one of her hands and kissed it. 'Darling,' he said, 'oh, darling. God, how I adore you.'

Now they were wholly together, now it was certain that their unity would persist and endure.

II

Next morning they walked together round the garden in the early light. Graham looked at everything with the intensity of conscious effort, the determination to have his memory accurate and sure. I shall always remember, he thought, the stonecrop on the walls, the colour of the roof, the distant Hampshire downs grey over the tops of the beeches, the odd shabby blue of the waterbutt by the scullery window. The morning sky was faint and cloudless, the air was cool. 'It's going to be a hot day,' said Deborah. They stood still and looked

at the cottage, both fixing this moment to hold against the future.

Faintly, so that at first they could believe it an illusion, they heard the engine of the village taxi that was to take Graham in to Winchester.

'He's dead on time,' he said, looking at his watch. 'My stuff is all down, isn't it?'

He put his arms round her, buried his mouth in her neck. 'Darling,' he half sobbed, 'darling, it's going to be all right, isn't it? Darling, we won't let anything spoil it, will we?'

Deborah whispered wildly, 'I promise you it will be all right. I love you, I love you, I don't want anyone else ever. Darling, I promise you, you've not got to worry about me at all. I'll wait for you, and I'll be happy waiting, I promise you, darling, it's worth it.'

For a moment they stood silent. Then he said, 'I'm not going to say goodbye to Timmy. He liked yesterday, and I don't want him to remember saying goodbye to me. God bless you both, darling. Maybe it won't be for long.'

He moved away from her, saluted her with an awkward rigid smile and went.

III

When the noise of Graham's taxi had died away, Deborah's first sensation was of relief. The strain of his embarkation leave had been almost intolerable, and now that he had inevitably gone, the release from emotional tension was

immediate. She had plenty to do. Mrs Chalmers, her mother's help, dealt with all the cooking and housework of the cottage, but in caring for Timmy, making his clothes, working in the garden, Deborah found her days sufficiently filled. Now that Graham had gone and her week's isolation with him was ended, there were again the normal social occupations of the village: the evening's bridge at the doctor's, the morning a week at the hospital canteen, the swopping over of children so that one or the other mother could get to see that new film in Winchester. Graham had gone, and the known monotony of her daily life was more than a comfort to Deborah. There was no opportunity for her to stop and bewail this separation for there was no one in the village from whom she could have expected sympathy; both the doctor's sons were away in the Navy; Betty Marsden had already lost her husband in France in 1940; Mrs Wendover's husband was safely in the North of Scotland, but she was held in the village by her house and her four children, and he hadn't been able to get south for the past six months. If Graham *had* to go off and leave me, Deborah said to herself, I think this is far and away the best place to be left in.

It was not until the end of August that Deborah's content began to break up. Each autumn in wartime, everyone is slightly more depressed than they were each spring, for they look forward to cold and black-out and bombing, and another Christmas of war. They have forgotten the fantastic hopes they entertained as the last winter faded away, or, if they remember them, it is only to contrast their past expectations with present reality.

So by the end of August Deborah was restless and bored. Her temper was ragged, and Timmy's reiterated and monotonous questions began to make her snap angrily at him, to cry, 'Shut up!' or in a fretful voice, 'Please stop talking, Timmy, Mummy just can't stand it,' and then to feel for herself all the pity she irrationally expected of the two-year-old Timmy. It was even a relief when one evening she had a trunk-call from her mother to say that she had just finished fitting her new clothes in London, and would like to come and spend a weekend with Deborah before going back to Leeds.

There had not been, for the last ten years, so much a state of enmity as of irritation between Mrs Ernest Betts and her daughter. Each looked on the other's standards with convinced contempt, and each, unfortunately, was possessed of a certain proselytising zeal that made nothing more difficult than to leave inviolate another person's point of view. During their struggle for supremacy Ernest Betts had died almost unnoticed, save as a counter in argument for whichever protagonist could drag his name in first. Ernest Betts had been a schoolboy in Leeds, a merchant in Leeds, and latterly a town councillor. His wife, who had met him in the first stage and buried him in the last, found such a life orderly and admirable. She had wanted nothing different for Deborah and was thoroughly annoyed when her daughter, on leaving school, had declared that she had an aptitude for art that only a course at the Slade could fulfil.

Mrs Betts was not altogether unperceptive. Had Deborah wanted the Slade as an ultimate enrichment of a life similar to her own, Mrs Betts would have raised no protest. She had

always had her communal work to fall back on and Deborah might just as well have had art. Equally, had Mrs Betts been assured that Deborah wanted the Slade because she must paint and couldn't live without paint, Mrs Betts would have been wholly sympathetic, for the reverence of most provincial citizens towards genuine art is altogether admirable. But Mrs Betts was no fool and she knew that Deborah wanted to go to the Slade for one reason only, and that was to marry out of the provinces into a better social position.

And she pulled it off all right, reflected her mother, jolting towards Deborah in the bus. Took her two years' fees at the Slade, but she pulled it off. Not that young Graham's got anything like as much money as she could have picked up at home, though I suppose an architect seems more high-falutin' to her ladyship than a successful business man. Doesn't to me, I must say, and mentally she priced the admirable and styleless garments she had just bought in London, and decided once again that life as the widow of a Leeds councillor was just about as good a life as could be lived.

Deborah was waiting for her at the Leather Bottle when the Winchester bus pulled in. She kissed her mother with unusual fervour, and said, 'Darling, I'm so glad you've come. I've been so lonely.'

'You look a bit off colour,' stated her mother, looking with surprise and some disfavour at Deborah's tired and pallid face, grubby sweater, and baggy tweed skirt. She decided not to enlarge on the subject yet, but asked, 'Where's Timmy?'

'He's out to tea with Betty Marsden's brats,' Deborah

replied wearily, 'I thought we'd fetch him on our way home.' She picked up her mother's zipped travelling bag. 'Is this all you've got?'

'Yes, I left the rest in the cloakroom at Winchester station,' said Mrs Betts. 'Well, let's be getting along. I haven't seen my grandson for over a year. Not much chance of him recognising me, I'm afraid.'

The two women walked up the village street in silence. They had never developed the art of meaningless small-talk with each other; virtually all their talks together had been fraught with deep personal significance and both, secretly delighting in and openly deprecating their emotional orgies, instinctively left these to a time when they could be pursued at leisure with no possibility of their being cut short by outside interference.

They picked up Timothy and continued their way to the cottage. Mrs Betts critically appraised her grandson. A year ago she had seen a rosy robust baby sitting triumphantly on the floor, crowing with uncontrollable delight at everything; now Timothy was thin and pale and uncertain of himself. He chattered constantly, but with no real gaiety, always glancing sideways towards his mother and then determinedly talking again.

Mrs Chalmers was waiting for them in the hall of the cottage. 'How nice to see you again, Mrs Betts,' she said pleasantly, and there was something in the way she said it that made Mrs Betts look sharply at her and decide that a few minutes' chat in the kitchen might not be time wasted. Mrs Chalmers added, 'Shall I put Timmy to bed for you tonight, Mrs Robertson? I'm sure you're longing to have a real nice talk with your mother.'

Deborah wearily assented, and her mother, following her into the sitting-room, heard Timmy going upstairs, saying in a voice entirely different from the one he had used on the walk home, 'Do you know, Mo, Pam gave me two chocolates after tea,' and Mrs Chalmers replying with apparently sincere interest, 'And did they have toffee middles or were they chocolate all the way through?' Deborah shut the door and said, 'I'm sorry I haven't anything to offer you, but it's practically impossible to get any drinks with Graham away.'

'I've brought you a bottle of sherry, it's in my bag,' said Mrs Betts. Deborah, with the first animation her mother had seen, said, 'Oh, good show,' and went for glasses and a corkscrew, while Mrs Betts produced the bottle.

Deborah began to look a little less tired. She questioned her mother eagerly about London, the shops, the restaurants. Mrs Betts said in surprise, 'But haven't you been up to town lately?'

'How can I?' said Deborah impatiently, 'I've got Timmy to see to, haven't I?'

'Mrs Chalmers looks very capable,' Mrs Betts mentioned tentatively, 'and Timmy seems very fond of her.'

'Oh, she's all right.' Deborah was sulky. 'She drives me absolutely mad most of the time. She's always yattering in that awful cheerful voice. It's all right for you to come on a visit and see how nice and helpful she is, but you'd go mad too if you had to sit with her every evening of your life and listen to the most godawful programmes on the radio or hear

her flat voice droning on about the late lamented husband in the Merchant Navy.'

Mrs Betts thought drily that those evenings must also be extremely trying for Mrs Chalmers, but she politely changed the subject and asked, 'And what do you hear from Graham?'

An uncontrollable spasm of vicious jealousy passed over Deborah's face. 'He seems to be having a marvellous time,' she said bitterly, 'moonlight picnics in the desert and sherry-parties and dances and what-not.' She looked across at her mother and burst out, 'I tell you it's almost unendurable, thinking of him away in the sun, seeing new places and people and going to parties and things, while I'm stuck here. And I know I ought to write him nice long cheerful letters about the happy home he's left behind and what-not, and I simply can't. I'm too miserable. Most of the time I just wish I were dead.'

There was a knock at the door and Mrs Chalmers' voice saying brightly, 'Timmy wants to say good night to Mummy and Grannie.' The women obediently filed upstairs, heard the baby's prayers, kissed him, and then came down again to supper.

Over the cold meat and salad, Mrs Betts and Mrs Chalmers kept up a bright flow of trivial small-talk, while Deborah glowered in her chair at their self-conscious, self-righteous acceptance of the situation's social demands. When the meal was over, Mrs Chalmers said, 'Well, seeing as you're both going to be in, you won't mind if I run across to Miss Langham? She's having a sewing-party and she's promised to show me

how to make those nice felt bedroom slippers. I'll wash up before I go.'

Settled in their armchairs drinking coffee, both women tacitly decided not to have a serious talk that evening. So Deborah politely asked after her old schoolfellows in Leeds and learnt without emotion or interest that Moira had married that nice young doctor, and Jean had had twins, while Mrs Betts tucked away the information that Graham's parents, who had gone to New York in 1940, had now moved on to friends in California and were proposing to stay there till the war was over; 'clears the decks,' was her mental comment, and at ten o'clock, feeling no further progress could be made till after the kitchen talk with Mrs Chalmers, she went up to bed.

Deborah and her mother had an instinctive understanding of each other's needs. Deborah, knowing perfectly that her mother was prepared to help her yet required as a preliminary the confidential talk behind her daughter's back, said next morning at breakfast, 'Mummy, I hope you don't mind, but I'd made an appointment to get my hair done in Winchester this morning; I'll be back for lunch.' The statement was so expected that the three women looked down at the tablecloth, fearing the embarrassment of understanding in each other's eyes.

IV

'Mind you, I'm very fond of Mrs Robertson,' said Mrs Chalmers self-righteously, 'and I'd do anything I could to

help her, but I can't think it's right her moping round the place like this. It's not as if it was doing Timmy any good, either.'

Both women looked at the child with passionate protectiveness. Already he had become the moral rock to which their tacit conspiracy was anchored.

'Do you yourself find the work here very hard?' Mrs Betts asked as if irrelevantly.

Mrs Chalmers understood her. 'I could do a great deal more and glad to, if only Mrs Robertson would let me,' she said. 'Many's the time I've said to her, now, Mrs Robertson, I've said, you just lie in bed this morning, and I'll bring your breakfast up to you and see to everything, but no, she won't have it, and after a while you don't feel like offering to do anything extra, not when you know your offer's going to be thrown back in your face, as it were.'

'Poor Deborah always was rather nervy,' said Mrs Betts, 'but I do know how much she appreciates having you here, Mrs Chalmers. Indeed, I don't know what she'd have done without you.'

'Oh, I can make all allowances,' Mrs Chalmers said, 'I know what it's like to have your husband away and not know from one day to the next whether he's safe or no. But I'm a different sort from Mrs Robertson, I daresay. Give me a good hard job to do so that I haven't got any time to sit and brood, and I can keep my feelings under.'

'I do agree with you,' said Mrs Betts firmly. The conversation was going just as she had hoped. 'I always felt that Deborah would be happiest with a job of work to keep her going. Naturally, one had hoped that Timmy would have been the job, but there,' she sighed, 'things don't always turn out as one intends, do they?'

'If I may say straight out what I think, Mrs Betts,' said Mrs Chalmers, 'I don't think Mrs Robertson is what I might call the mother type.'

Momentarily the conversation hung suspended. Once it went on there could be no turning back.

Mrs Betts said, 'I'm afraid I agree with you. In a great many ways, I'm sorry she had the baby so soon. If it wasn't for him, I'm quite convinced that the best thing she could have done would have been to have taken a job somewhere, and felt she was really doing something towards the war. It's not doing her or the child any good, her staying here and feeling thwarted and unhappy.'

'But Mrs Betts –' said Mrs Chalmers eagerly. The matter was settled.

V

'Well,' said Mrs Chalmers, 'I'll just take these things along and get washed up.' She carried away the coffee-tray with ostentatious tactfulness, leaving Deborah and Mrs Betts tensed in their armchairs.

Mrs Betts pulled some khaki knitting from a quilted chintz bag. 'If you don't mind, dear,' she said gently, 'I think I'll get on with my scarf while we talk. I find I can concentrate so much better when my hands are occupied.'

Deborah said pettishly, 'I can't see there's anything to talk

about. I've got no alternative, I've just got to stay here and rot till the war's over, and no amount of talking can alter that.'

'Why have you got to?' asked Mrs Betts.

'Well, there's Timmy, isn't there?' said Deborah sulkily and looked hopefully at her mother.

Mrs Betts laid her knitting on her lap. 'Well,' she said carefully, 'I've been wondering if you really are doing the right thing for Timothy by staying here.'

'Why?' asked Deborah coldly.

Now, said Mrs Betts to herself, I must be very very careful indeed; if I once antagonise her, it's all up. She said, 'I know, Deborah, that you've thought for a long time that I judge you too harshly. I think, perhaps, before you were married I did, because it's rather difficult for a mother to understand a daughter who has taken an altogether different path from herself. But I want you to know I really do understand now that you had to do the things you did to develop your own personality.' Am I laying it on too thick, she wondered, but Deborah's face, if expressionless, was not antagonistic. She went on. 'And that's why, after you've had all the struggle to express yourself and develop yourself, it seems rather a shame to watch you just throwing it all away.'

Deborah believed this, but was distrustful of her mother saying it. She commented with a sneer, 'I never thought I'd hear you say that staying at home to look after one's dear little baby was throwing oneself away.'

Mrs Betts tried to say humbly, 'Well, it wouldn't have been for me. But I was brought up so differently from you. I never had the chance to find out whether there was, perhaps, some

other job I'd have done better, so I just turned to, and did the one that lay in hand. But just because one's had a child isn't any reason for one to be the best person to look after it, particularly in wartime when there's probably another job one could do infinitely better.'

Deborah said aggressively, 'So you think I'm bad for my own child?'

I've got to take each point patiently, said Mrs Betts to herself; it's got to be talked out, once and for all. She said, 'If I may speak frankly, Deborah, that's just what I do think. I don't mean this for any disparagement of you, but I do think that there are fundamentally two types of women in the world, the mother type and the – the wife type.' She hesitated over the last epithet, unable to say the word that was really in her mind. 'And I don't think you are really the first sort. I'm quite sure that when Graham is home, the baby is secondary to your life with him. Isn't that so?'

Deborah, turning over this new, potentially constructive idea, said 'Yes.'

Mrs Betts went on, 'As you know, I've never had any patience with psycho-analysts and all their mumbo-jumbo. But I can see that if a woman is not a mother type, first and foremost, she's not likely, with her husband away, to be the very best person to look after her own baby. Without Graham, what you really need is a full-time job to occupy you and keep you happy and contented, and then, when you saw your baby, he'd have the best of you, not the worst.'

'What job could I do?' Deborah demanded.

'Well,' Mrs Betts temporised, 'there's lots of things going

on in Winchester, aren't there, and with your abilities you should easily find something to suit you.'

'Not Winchester.' Deborah flung the town contemptuously away. 'All the decent jobs have gone to canons' wives and people like that, and in any case they're all voluntary. The only paid jobs going are for clerks. No, if I *was* going to take a job, at least I'd go to London and take a proper job in one of the Ministries like most of my friends have done.'

This was going rather further than Mrs Betts had intended. Without evoking a definite picture that needs must be rejected, she knew instinctively what must happen to Deborah if she went to London.

'You wouldn't be able to get home every night to see Timmy,' she suggested hesitantly.

Deborah had now taken a firm hold of her mother's tentative suggestion. 'That idea would be agony,' she said decisively, 'I couldn't endure rushing home every night only just in time to kiss him good night, and then rushing off first thing in the morning. No, if I *am* going to work, it's much better to have a clean break and not get Timmy emotionally upset, spending all day longing for me to come home.'

Mrs Betts silently agreed that the pull of Deborah's evening emotions might be extremely bad for Timmy, but still she had hardly envisaged so complete a change in Deborah's life; London in wartime, she said to herself, is a very different cup of tea from Winchester. 'Where would you live?' she asked.

Deborah tossed the question away. 'Oh, there's Madeleine Crayshaw has got a flat I could share, or I could go into digs

with Mary Burns, or one of the others,' she said. 'What's much more difficult is what I'm going to live *on*. I've hardly got enough to keep two establishments going, you know.'

Without meaning to, Mrs Betts said swiftly, 'You know, I'd love to take Timmy back to Leeds with me.' She stopped, dismayed; now I've ruined it all, she thought.

But Deborah was too much enamoured of the scheme as a whole to wreck it on details. 'I don't really think that would do,' she said gently, 'I feel absolutely convinced that Graham would loathe to think of Timmy being brought up anywhere but in his own house.'

And what would Graham think of your leaving him here and going gallivanting off to London, wondered Mrs Betts grimly, but she was too wise now to wonder aloud. Instead she said, 'In that case, I wonder if you'd let me pay Mrs Chalmers' wages for you? Then you could afford on your allowance to pay for her and Timmy's keep, and you'd have a bit over, together with whatever you earn, to keep yourself.'

Deborah accepted without comment the news that Mrs Chalmers was prepared wholly to take over her own responsibilities; but this setting out of the situation in concrete terms of money roused a momentary panic in her. She cried, 'Mummy, do you really think I'd be right to go?'

Mrs Betts had feared this all along. As always, when a final decision had to be made, Deborah wanted to push the ultimate responsibility of it on to someone else, and preferably on to her mother. Then, if things went wrong, she would be able to say, 'I never really wanted to do this, but my mother forced me into it.'

And am I prepared for her to say that in this case, Mrs Betts asked herself. I can see quite clearly what will happen to her if she goes to live in London – but I can see equally well the irremediable harm she will do my baby if she stops here. The question is, which is the more important to me, my daughter or my grandson? Do I mind more if my daughter goes to the bad or my grandson has his nerves upset and his character ruined?

She said firmly, 'I think you'd be wronging yourself if you didn't go. You've got talents and you'd only be wasting yourself; you'd not be doing your duty in wartime if you didn't use them.'

Deborah's whole face altered. Suddenly she looked young, ardent, beautiful. 'God Almighty,' she breathed in heartfelt uncontrollable ecstasy of release.

CHAPTER TWO

❦❦❦❦❦

So one morning the following week, Deborah went up to London to see about getting a job. 'I'll be back on the late train,' she had said to Mrs Chalmers, 'I don't suppose I'll actually find anything the first time I go, but there's no harm in having a look round.' Mrs Chalmers had agreed as, on Mrs Betts' advice, she was able to agree to anything Deborah said these days, so long as it would bring closer her ultimate possession of Timmy.

The departure had been a little marred by Timmy's sudden sobs at the prospect of his mother's leaving, and his wild entreaties to be taken too. But, said Deborah, who was now able to see everything the way she wished it, that only shows how bad it is for a child to get emotionally dependent on one person; however much it may hurt me, I owe it to Timmy to release him from me. It was in a glow of maternal renunciation that she got into the train and jolted uncomfortably up to London.

She had already written to Madeleine Crayshaw to say that she was coming up and suggesting a lunch date, and Madeleine had replied fixing the Berkeley Buttery at one. Deborah took a bus from Waterloo to Bond Street and then walked slowly towards Piccadilly.

London began to intoxicate her. She looked with ecstasy at the hats in the shop windows, the women on the pavements, the important cars rolling up and down the street. I must have been mad, she said to herself, to give it up for so long. She was not the type to feel awkward or self-conscious at her own shabby tweeds, her flat shoes, her useful felt hat; she ignored these, completely confident that they were only the chrysalis from which she would presently emerge. When she walked into the Buttery Bar and saw Madeleine, sleek and immaculate in black, her reaction was not one of inferiority, but confidence born of the assurance of how much nicer than Mady she would look, when she, too, got into that uniform of a woman about town.

Madeleine Crayshaw was four or five years older than Deborah. She came of a poverty-stricken county family in Cheshire, and, like Deborah, had used the excuse of an urge for art to escape from it. But, unlike Deborah, she had never deceived herself into believing that art was really the urge that had brought her to London. She had attended the barest minimum of classes at the Slade, and spent the rest of the time building up a social life remarkable for its complete contrast with her former life at home. It was at a party in Mady's pre-war flat in Wellington Square, Chelsea, that Deborah had met Graham. Madeleine had herself acquired a husband shortly before the war began, but the marriage was known to be a failure, and Edward's departure to Burma with his regiment seemed to be regretted by no one.

She waved a cigarette at Deborah as she came in. 'I've ordered a Bronx for you,' she said, 'I hope you can drink it.

I had to order something to convince the girl that I really needed it to keep another chair. Well, how's the Hampshire countryside?'

'Bloody awful,' said Deborah, sitting down and drinking her cocktail; I don't believe I've had one since Graham went away, she thought in surprise. She asked reciprocally, 'And how's the job going?'

Madeleine said, 'My dear, it's the most immense sport. I'm the only woman – a sort of junior filing-clerk in a minute office, occupied by four stalwart men. Two of them are dons torn from their colleges and utterly terrifying, but rather pets.'

'What sort of work is it?' Deborah asked curiously.

'Terribly hush-hush,' Mady whispered mysteriously, 'and utterly puerile,' she ended. 'Well, come on, let's go and eat while there's still a chance of a table.'

Over their grilled herring, Madeleine remembered to ask 'Well, how's the small son – or is it a daughter?'

'He's terribly sweet,' said Deborah, resisting an impulse to tell Madeleine the really brilliant remark he had made in his bath the previous night. Remembering Timmy with an acute spasm of tenderness, she told herself in panic that she wasn't committed to anything as yet, then heard Madeleine saying, 'And what exactly has brought you up to town? I had the impression you were wholly absorbed in the cares of hearth and home.'

The image of Timmy's firm rosy body receded a little. Deborah said, 'I was really wondering, Mady, if it wouldn't be a good idea if I took a job in London to keep myself occupied till Graham gets back.'

Madeleine had known her moments of self-questioning and disgust. Madeleine had known herself envying Deborah with a fervid bitterness. Now she thought contemptuously, so I was really right, there's damn-all in this home and infant stuff after all, and with that thought came a strong almost unconscious desire to prove to Deborah that she, Madeleine, had been right all along, that her way of life was altogether the better one; perhaps I could really be sure of it myself then, she thought, and she said, 'And what happens to the infant?'

Deborah said eagerly, 'I've got an absolutely marvellous housekeeper who simply adores him. She's longing to take him over altogether, and honestly, I think she'd be much better for him than I would. I'm all edgy and nervy, and I do really think it would be far better for Timmy if I had a job that occupied my thoughts and kept me from brooding all the time.'

Madeleine said drily, 'I should think it probably would be. Have you any particular job in mind?'

'I wondered if you could get me anything in your office?' Deborah asked. Madeleine said, 'I should think it highly probable. We're always taking in new people. But mind you, it would only be a stooge job like mine, and the pay is quite lousy. Three quid a week is good for a start.'

'I shouldn't mind that,' said Deborah, 'I've got about two hundred a year from Graham after I've paid for Timmy and Mrs Chalmers. The difficulty would be to find somewhere to live during the week. You see, I'd be going home every weekend.'

'Well, if you're seriously interested, I'll certainly do what I can,' Madeleine assured her. 'When are you going back to Winchester?'

'I was thinking of doing a bit of shopping, and then catching the 6.05.'

Madeleine said quickly, 'Oh, don't do that. Stay the night and we'll have a party. I can give you a sofa to sleep on.'

Deborah hesitated. 'I don't think I can stay overnight,' she said. 'I promised Timmy I'd be back by the time he woke up in the morning. But I must say, it would be fun to see a bit of life. I could catch the nine something after dinner.'

'Well, stay for dinner anyway,' said Madeleine, 'and we'll see how the evening goes. I'll get hold of a couple of men, and we'll go to Quags, or somewhere. Do you think you could roll up at my flat round about six?'

II

Deborah paced Dover Street till she found a hairdresser who could make her hair look a little more like London, and less like the provinces. She had a face treatment and emerged with an exotic make-up. I can't do anything about my clothes she told herself, slipping her felt hat into her shopping bag, but it's not as if it mattered. I mean, I'm quite sure Graham wouldn't mind me just going out to dinner and dancing a bit; it's not as if anything was going to come of it.

She walked confidently into Madeleine's Hallam Street flat soon after six. Its decoration impressed her, with its concealed lighting, its heavy velvet curtains, its deep armchairs.

Madeleine, who was mixing drinks, explained, 'I got it furnished from a man in the BBC who's gone to the States. I know it looks rather a tart-trap, but it's comfortable and I don't have to do anything about keeping it clean. I share it with another girl who's working in the Foreign Office, but she has a bed sitting-room of her own next door, and we both like living privately so it works out rather well.'

Deborah asked, 'Who's coming tonight?'

Madeleine, pouring out a drink for Deborah answered, 'Robert Mannington-Smith. He works at the Admiralty. He's mine, by the way. He's bringing a man called Peter Naughton who's wildly attractive but just not my type, so he's yours for the asking.'

Deborah said priggishly, 'I'm not exactly man-hunting, just now.'

'No,' said Madeleine, with raised eyebrows.

'No,' said Deborah firmly. The doorbell rang and Madeleine went to answer it. 'Here they are,' she said, coming back with the two men. 'Deborah, the fair one is Robert, and the dark one is Peter, and this is Deborah Robertson, who has emerged from the country and wants to have a night out.'

'Within the limits of a train at nine-something,' said Deborah.

'Shame,' cried Peter Naughton. 'No one can have a night out between 6 pm and nine-something. I shall feel seriously insulted if you manage to catch it.'

'You can feel inordinately flattered if I don't,' Deborah said. She looked at his uniform. 'What sort of ship are you in, or is that a deadly secret?'

'I think I can safely say, don't you, Robert? Robert's my official superior,' he explained, 'and I have to be very very careful when he's about. Anyway, I'll risk my career and tell you. I work in a destroyer, which is a very swift and very deadly ship.'

'Any ship you were on would be pretty deadly,' Madeleine interrupted. 'Have a drink. Robert, a drink?'

Peter sat on the arm of Deborah's chair. He picked up her hand and began playing with it so idly that she had no excuse for pulling it away. He said, 'I was really feeling exceptionally browned off before we came here. I'd just been told that we've got to be prepared to depart for a distant destination at unreasonably short notice. So you see, it's really your duty to cheer the departing mariner.'

Deborah looked at Peter. He was as tritely tall, dark and handsome as those adjectives imply. In addition, he was gay and confident and attractive. 'I'll do my best,' she said. 'Mady, is there another drink going before you swipe the lot?'

III

They had some more drinks at the Ritz to fill in time, and then some more drinks at Quaglino's to fill in more time before the table Robert had booked was ready for them. By that time it was half-past eight, and Deborah, sufficiently drunk to feel very gay and extraordinarily attractive, had secretly decided that she wasn't going to mention her train until somebody else did. Someone is sure to, she told herself, but nobody did, and by the time it would have been necessary to leave in order to catch it, she had forgotten it herself.

They had a table for four against the wall, but after they had ordered their food, the party split up. Peter and Deborah danced with each other, and held hands together in the intervals of dancing, and eventually Peter whispered to Deborah, 'Let's ditch the others and go and dance privately. I've had a flat lent to me, and there's a bottle of whisky in it.' Deborah looked at Madeleine, who, just then, was most competently raising her eyes to meet Robert's. Peter added urgently, 'They don't want us. I'll settle with old Robert in the morning,' and Deborah, now wholly excited and drunk, slipped out with him.

The flat was somewhere off Baker Street. Peter pushed her gently in and switched on the radio. Deborah flung herself on to a large untidy divan that lay near the spluttering gas fire. She felt full of life and vigour yet, at the same time, languorous and expectant. She had no conscious thought but a strong sensation that she was somehow absolved from all responsibility. Peter came to bring her a glass of whisky. She had never liked the taste of whisky before, but now it seemed to intensify everything, to make her sense of irresponsibility a responsibility in itself. Peter put his empty glass carefully on to the floor and pulled her towards him. 'You're rather sweet, you know,' he said heavily in her ear.

IV

The black-out curtains shone greyly with the morning light that filtered through them. Deborah awoke, sickeningly aware that something was horribly wrong. The gas fire was still spluttering noisily and in its light Deborah could see the empty

glass, the full ash-trays, her coat that had slipped on to the floor, her clothes over the big armchair and Peter Naughton's head on the soiled divan cushion beside her. Moving with desperate caution, Deborah slid from under the rug that had covered them both, and on to the floor. Her mouth was parched and sore, and her head ached with a dull sickening leadenness. She began to put on her clothes.

Disconcertingly she discovered that Peter was awake and watching her. He said, 'What's the hurry, darling? It's warmer in bed.'

Deborah, pulling on her skirt with desperate untidy haste, said, 'You're revolting.' She had not meant to say this, but it was so forcefully in her mind it had to come out.

Peter raised himself on his elbow and said, 'Having a hangover, sweetie pie? You're being a little insulting, you know. You didn't find me exactly revolting last night.'

Deborah was trying to button her frock with fingers that persisted in finding the wrong buttonhole. She said distractedly, longing only to be gone, 'I don't mean you were revolting, it's just – oh God, it's the whole set-up, it's not your fault.'

Peter said as if with interest. 'And what exactly is so revolting about the whole set-up?'

Deborah had fastened her skirt now and felt less vulnerable. She said, picking up her bag, 'I suppose it's you not loving me that makes the whole thing seem just filthy.'

'Oh, you're one of those,' said Peter, and lay back on the cushions, roaring with laughter.

Now Deborah was disconcerted, thinking she had made a statement personal to herself and finding instead that it branded her as one of a type that made Peter roar with laughter. She said angrily, 'I don't see anything funny in suggesting that it's filthy to go to bed with people who aren't in love with one.'

Peter said, 'Look here, darling, if you're a girl-friend of Madeleine's, it's time you learnt something about the facts of life. I don't go to bed with people because I'm in love with them; I go to bed with people because I want them. Girls who want men to be in love with them first are girls who want to tie strings on men, and I'm not buying that one. Don't be a little fool. You wanted it last night as much as I did, and it's no good telling me this morning that you feel all wronged because I didn't love you; frankly, that line of talk doesn't mean a thing to me.'

Deborah could find no answer. She thought that she was standing on an unassailable right in her demand for love before immorality. That this tenet should be mocked at, even held against her, left her wholly discomposed. She picked up her bag and moved towards the door.

Peter said coaxingly, 'You're rather fun, you know. Why not lie up a bit and get over your hangover, and we'll go places tonight?'

Deborah from the door said, 'You're utterly and entirely revolting, and I hope to God I never see you again.' She opened the door and went out, remembering to close it softly behind her lest someone else in the building should look out of their door to see who was leaving so early in the morning, and should, by a fatal chance, be someone who knew her.

V

The air in Portman Square was cool and clean. Deborah looked at her watch and saw that it was half-past five. She decided to walk to Waterloo and catch the first train that would take her back to Timmy and cleanliness and security.

How could I have done it, she asked herself distractedly, I meant to be faithful to Graham, honestly I did, please don't let it count against me, don't let anything happen to Timmy, don't let Graham be unfaithful to me because of it. She walked swiftly, trying by physical movement to dull the wild prayers that rose in her, God, don't let it count against me, you know I didn't mean to do it, it didn't mean a thing to me, it was just that I was drunk, and Graham's been away so long. At this point a voice in her mind said firmly, Graham's going to be away a good deal longer, and frantically she prayed, God, I won't ever do it again, so long as you don't count it against me, don't spoil things because of it, I'm not really wicked, it's just – and on she walked, praying and arguing and bargaining till she reached Waterloo.

The next train, she was told, was at 7.25. Deborah sat alone on a bench at the end of the almost deserted station feeling more unhappy and forlorn than ever in her life before. At last the cold fuggy train pulled in and Deborah climbed heavily into an empty third-class compartment and, huddled up on the seat, tried to sleep.

On the country bus she thought, I can't tell Mrs Chalmers I came back on the 7.25, she'd think something was phoney straight away. She began to make up a story, a party, the late

train from London, no more buses out, knocked up friends in Jewry Street, left first thing.

Mrs Chalmers had been worried, so worried in fact, that in telling over the details of her worry she had hardly time to listen to Deborah's story. 'Should I ring up Mrs Betts, I asked myself,' she said, 'not knowing who to get in touch with, though I listened to the seven o'clock and the eight o'clock and they both said no enemy action last night, though one never knows and they say there's more deaths from road accidents than bombs anyway. Till ten o'clock I was going to give you, and then I really don't know what I'd have done.'

Deborah broke in with, 'Where's Timmy?'

Mrs Chalmers explained, 'Little Elizabeth Marsden came round, only five minutes ago it was, and said could he come and play with them, so I let him go and glad to, not knowing what I might be called on to do. But there, you're safe and sound, though it was a pity you couldn't telephone me; still, as you say, a telephone call at midnight would have scared the life out of me as likely as not. Have you had anything for breakfast, Mrs Robertson, or would you like me to fry you up some bacon? It won't take a jiffy.'

Deborah's stomach turned in disgust. She managed to say politely, 'I'm not really hungry, thank you, though I'd love it if you'll make me some really strong coffee. I think I'll just go and have a bath if the water's hot.'

'Piping hot,' said Mrs Chalmers proudly. She wondered whether to ask Mrs Robertson if she'd had any success in looking for a job, then decided it wasn't the moment. Really worn out she looks, she said to herself, and no wonder, travelling being what it is nowadays. She turned to the kitchen stove.

Deborah poured a generous dose of Dettol into the bath, and meticulously scrubbed herself all over. She ran herself another bath, perfumed it, and lay there deciding what was best to think.

The first thing to decide, she said to herself, is, must I tell Graham about this?

She remembered her passionate assertions to him before he left. If *I* can be faithful, she had said in effect, why can't *you*? But now, at the very first test, Deborah had found that she couldn't be, and, if she confessed that to Graham, might he not take it as justifying a similar disregard of fidelity for himself? And it's not, said Deborah, as if this time ought to count, I mean, I lost my head and I had too much to drink and I just didn't know how easy the temptation was. Nobody blames anyone for getting drunk when they've never had anything to drink before and just doesn't know what it does to them. Well, it was exactly like that, wasn't it? Next time I'd know where I was going, and then it *would* be wrong, but I don't see how anyone could blame me when I just didn't understand where I was going. If Graham was here I could tell him about it and he'd understand, but those things seem so different when they're written down. Besides, it would be rather too low to ease my own conscience just at the expense of making Graham miserable when he's miles away, and can't do anything about it anyway. No, she said, melodramatically to herself, I must bear the burden of my guilt alone and I suppose that will be my punishment.

Enormously relieved by her decision, Deborah got dressed. 'I'm going to fetch Timmy,' she said gaily to Mrs Chalmers, and walked down the village street, full of longing for her unjudging, adoring baby.

'The children are in the garden,' Betty Marsden said, 'come along,' and she led Deborah out.

Timmy and the two Marsden children were squatting on a heap of sand. Each had some sort of receptacle which was being carefully filled with a wooden spoon, emptied out and refilled again. The two women stood watching them for a while, then Deborah, unable to resist the desire to break Timmy's absorption into pleasure at her return, called out to him.

Exactly as she had hoped, he looked up and saw her, momentary incredulity replaced with intense delight. He struggled to his feet, dropping his toys, and started to run to her.

But just before he reached her, he checked himself. He put his thumb into his mouth and stood still, glancing uneasily at his mother out of the corner of his eye.

Deborah, aghast, cried, 'Darling, it's Mummy come back again. Come to Mummy, darling,' but still Timmy stood there and sucked his thumb.

Betty Marsden, who liked reading books on child psychology, explained detachedly. 'He's distrustful of you, of course, because you went away from him, and he doesn't like to entrust his security to you again now you've shown that you're not wholly tied to him and his desires. I remember–' but Deborah had rushed to her son and was kneeling on

the grass, trying to enfold his small resistant figure in her arms.

'Darling, darling,' she whispered passionately to him, 'Mummy's come back, darling, Mummy's not going to go away again ever, Mummy's going to stay with her baby.' Timmy softened, and fell against her and Deborah gripped him tightly and whispered into his hair, 'I promise you, darling, Mummy will stay with you always.'

VI

That evening after supper, Mrs Chalmers asked, 'And how did you find London?'

Deborah replied shortly, 'It's horribly shabby and crowded. I was delighted to get home again.'

Mrs Chalmers doggedly pursued. 'And did you have any luck in looking for a job?'

Deborah was always antagonistic to queries about her movements. Remembering her mother and her childhood, she felt that such questions were an attempt to establish control over her. She said in an off-hand voice, 'Well I didn't really try very hard. I'm afraid the prospect of working up there didn't appeal so much as Timmy,' and, not bothering to look at the sudden disappointment on Mrs Chalmers' face, she fetched some note-paper and a pen and prepared to compose a thank-you letter to Madeleine.

I must tell her, she thought, her pen scribbling lines on the blotting paper, that I've definitely given up all idea of a job in London; I don't want her to bother to look for one when I don't want it. She wrote,

I loved seeing you again, and I enjoyed our evening a lot. You can imagine what fun it was after months in the country. I was sorry I had to rush away, but you know how things are.

That covers catching a train without telling any lies, she thought; and unless that man's told her all about it, I needn't bother to say anything. She wrote,

I do hope it won't be long before we see each other again. Love, Deborah

and put it quickly into an envelope without re-reading it.

VII

Timmy during the next few weeks gave Deborah unmixed satisfaction. He behaved to her with constant adoration, offering her his most precious toys, entreating her perpetual presence, wooing her by every means in his power, while Deborah basked in his admiration, telling herself constantly that here in her home with her child was the only wholly satisfactory life.

One day, during these weeks, a woman friend came out from Winchester to have tea with Deborah. 'Are you still looking for a job?' she asked, 'because if you are, I think I've heard of the very thing. You know that secret show that's working on Worthy Down? Well, I've just heard that they want a woman. I gather there's no typing or shorthand about it;

all they want is someone intelligent and discreet. The girl who told me about it works there, and she seems to find it quite fascinating.'

'What's the screw?' Deborah asked without much interest.

'Three ten, I think she said.'

'And the hours?'

'Oh,' said the friend, 'they're really very reasonable. Nine-thirty to six, and half-day Saturday and all Sunday free, which is really very good as so many jobs nowadays seem to mean working weekends. I thought of you right away, but if you're interested you'd better get on to them tomorrow at the latest, because if it gets known about it, there'll be plenty of people after it. I'll leave you the name of the man you have to go and see.'

The friend went back to Winchester and Deborah sat in front of the fire twisting in her hands the scrap of paper with the name of the man she would have to get on to by tomorrow at the latest. She wondered why she felt no enthusiasm for the job. Truly, as the friend had said, it seemed in every respect just what she wanted. She could not expect better hours or pay anywhere, and as she would be able to get home every evening, the pay would be all profit. It was generally known round Winchester just what the most secret organisation was doing, and it was far from uninteresting. I suppose, said Deborah, the reason I'm not interested is because I really want to stay at home with Timmy. She dropped the scrap of paper into the fire, and the weeks went by.

Just before Christmas she had a letter from Madeleine. It read,

Everything always seems to happen at once. I'd been keeping my ears open for you and nothing seemed to turn up, but yesterday a man I know in another Ministry told me he was looking for a new woman – they're not so easy to find nowadays. I should think the job is just what you want, interesting enough not to be too boring and not important enough to be a worry. Also, by the most amazing stroke of luck, Katherine, the girl who shares my flat, has been sent to India so if you'd like to come in like she did it would be grand. She paid me three quid, which is all your earnings, but you said the money wasn't all that important to you and I don't suppose your expenses will be much. This man wants to be fixed up by the New Year, so come up and see about it as soon as Christmas is over.

Deborah's instantaneous thought was, at least I can have Christmas with Timmy. Then she stopped aghast. Of course, there could be no question of her taking this job when she had already turned down a far better one, just because it would have taken her away from her baby. She must write to tell Madeleine at once and tell her firmly it was no use.

But before she did that she had to dash to the butcher to see if she could get a bit of liver. Then there were Timmy's clothes to wash and the table to lay for lunch and after lunch she had to read the new novel Mrs Wendover had lent her on condition she returned it that same evening. And then there were a couple of children to tea and after that, all the ceremony of putting Timmy to bed, and by that time the last post had gone, so there was really no hurry.

I must be sure to thank Mady very nicely, Deborah mused after dinner, she's really gone to an awful lot of trouble about me. I do feel rather a cad just throwing it back in her face.

She said impulsively to Mrs Chalmers, seated on the other side of the fire, 'I had a letter today from the friend I went to see in London. She says she's found me a job if I want it.'

Mrs Chalmers was surprised. She had accepted the situation that Deborah had given up all idea of going away and working, and, now that Deborah was being more even-tempered and amiable to Timothy, she didn't really mind. The child was genuinely her first interest, and she must look at every situation in that light. Now she said cautiously, 'And what do you feel about it?'

'Well,' said Deborah, 'it's an opportunity,' and as she said the words the prospect seemed to fall into a new perspective; opportunities made their moral demands.

'It certainly is that,' agreed Mrs Chalmers, who had fundamentally the same outlook on opportunities as Deborah; while opportunities that did not appeal could slide by unnoticed, it was immoral to disregard opportunities that did.

'My friend's been to a lot of trouble for me,' Deborah went on, 'I don't want to feel I'm letting her down.'

'No,' said Mrs Chalmers, 'one never likes to let people down, not when they've been to a lot of trouble.'

'How do you think Timmy would feel about it?' Deborah asked.

Mrs Chalmers thought hard about this. She wanted to give an honest answer.

'Well, children get used to anything,' she said at last. 'Of course he'd be in his own house with his own things and all the children he knows round about, and he'd quickly accept it. But there's no denying he'd be rather upset at first. He's got very fond of you just lately, you know, Mrs Robertson.'

'Too fond, perhaps,' said Deborah with a sigh. She wondered whether she'd been quite fair to Timmy, letting him get so dependent on her, when life demanded we should each stand on our own feet.

Mrs Chalmers hazarded tentatively, 'Of course, you could try it and see how it works out.'

'I suppose I could do that,' Deborah said, but she was not really convinced that this was practicable. Surely this job would be one of those you couldn't get away from even if you wanted to, and anyway, Madeleine would hardly want her to come and share her flat on a purely temporary basis.

Mrs Chalmers rolled up her knitting and put it away in its bag. 'Well, it certainly is an opportunity,' she remarked again, 'you want to think it over very carefully before you turn it down flat.'

In bed, Deborah thought it over as carefully as she could. I don't think, she decided, I need consider the question of sex and temptation and all that. I'm quite decided I won't let myself do anything like that again. If I was frightened I might do so, of course, I'd stay here where I'm safe, but I must think pretty poorly of my will-power if I'm afraid it will break down at the slightest temptation. I mean, it would

be rather cowardly to stay here just because I'm afraid of myself.

Then, she said, there's the question of Timmy. I rather think one's got to take the long view. Of course it would be nicer for him, and for me too, to stay together, but one's got to consider what's best for him, not what's nicest. It's no good bringing him up to a comfortable dependent security, that certainly doesn't exist nowadays and isn't likely to in the world he'll grow up in. Surely, however much it may hurt me, I owe it to my child to make him strong enough to face all knocks of life rather than to protect him against them?

That, said Deborah, is a painful conclusion, but all sacrifice is painful or it wouldn't be worth anything. The important thing is to see things straight and then face up to the sacrifices involved.

Lastly, she said, there is of course the question of patriotism, even though it isn't really a thing one talks about nowadays. I can't really, if I look at it honestly, feel it's justifiable in these times to have both Mrs Chalmers and myself looking after Timmy and this tiny cottage. Superficially, I suppose people would say I ought to let Mrs Chalmers go and cope with everything myself, but that wouldn't really help any-one. For one thing, if Mrs Chalmers left me, she wouldn't go into war work, she'd just take another post of exactly the same kind as this while I'd be left doing a job I loathe and am rotten at anyway. While if I go, and she stays here, I think I can honestly say that's a more valuable effort as far as the war goes. I mean, I'm not exactly a fool, and I'd be far more use to the country doing an interesting office job than I would making a mess of the housework.

I think that's everything, she said to herself, and I think I can see things clearly now. She thought she would go to sleep easily but for some hours she lay awake, repeating her arguments over to herself.

VIII

The next day Deborah wrote two letters. The first was to Madeleine and that was easy. The second was to Graham.

Darling, she wrote, I wish desperately you were here with me just now, because I've had to decide something rather difficult, and though I think I've decided rightly, I wish so much you were here to tell me so. But I've had to decide rather suddenly and there just wasn't time to wait for an answer from you.

The thing is this, I'm taking a job in London. An old school-friend knows someone in one of the Ministries who wants a girl to do some work that's just up my street and I've decided to go and do it. It was a horribly difficult thing to decide, as you can imagine, but leaving aside all considerations like patriotism and wanting to do something to help to get you home quickly, there's another and bigger reason, and that is the way I miss you. I just haven't got enough to think about here, nor enough to do, and I can't go on missing you the way I do. I feel that if I've got a full-time job to

occupy my thoughts, all that will be so much better. And I shall have all my weekends here with Timmy, so I shall be much better off than people like your cousin in the ATS who only sees her children when she's on leave.

Darling, she ended, I love you so much and only you, you know that, don't you? You know how much I miss you and how longingly I'm waiting for you to come back home.

IX

On Christmas Eve she took Timmy to the carol service in the village church. He was really too young for it, but Deborah was determined to wallow through Christmas in an orgy of sentimentality. As she stood him on the seat beside her and encouraged him to pipe such words as he knew, she wished fiercely that he should remember irrevocably this scene and its emotions, his mother's lovely face in her little fur bonnet, the blue-painted ceiling, the choristers' voices, the deeply pervading sadness of Christmas in wartime.

She took him home through the cold starlit night and put him to bed. As she pinned his sock on to the end of his cot, she felt an overpowering impulse to deepen the emotional intensity of this evening. She stood over Timmy and stroked his forehead and said, 'Timmy, after Christmas Mummy's got to go away.'

Timmy, not very interested, said, 'You going to Winchester?'

Deborah smiled sadly and said, 'No darling, Mummy's got to go further than Winchester, Mummy's going to London to help to win the war and bring Daddy home again quickly.'

Timmy said, 'When's Father Christmas going to come down the chimney?' and Deborah sighed deeply and turned away.

CHAPTER THREE

As soon as Christmas was over Deborah went up to London. She was interviewed by her future employer, who was a don of the type Deborah admired but disliked. He wanted her to start work the following Monday, five days ahead. Then she went to see Madeleine, looked at her bed sitting-room which was furnished with the same lavish vulgarity as the rest of the flat, and caught the nine-something home, arranging to move in on Sunday evening.

Now that there was no drawing back, a deep sadness took hold of Deborah. Life in the cottage with Timmy seemed infinitely pleasanter than anything that London could hold. More than that, it seemed safe and secure and all else seemed full of perils. During these last days the thought of starting her new life in London made Deborah's stomach contract in dread. 'I'd give it all up,' she said to herself more than once, 'if only it wouldn't make me look such a fool.'

So all those last days she lived passionately, fearfully, in every moment, constantly saying to herself, now I am here, now it is real, now I am touching Timmy and it is inconceivable that there'll come a moment when he is not with me for the touching, until that moment came and she was alone in her bed sitting-room on Sunday evening with no one to talk to and nothing to do.

Madeleine had said, 'William and I are going to the Savoy. Would you like to come along and eat with us and see who we run into?' but Deborah had refused, made herself a cup of tea and sat alone in the vulgar bed sitting-room.

During that first month she became accustomed to the routine of loneliness. She had to be at her job earlier than Madeleine, so she would get up and make herself a cup of tea and go to the office. There for the moment her loneliness was appeased. The work was interesting and seemed easy, the girls were friendly and uncompetitive and were there to be talked to for the eleven o'clock break and the lunch in the canteen. But inevitably the day ended and Deborah would go back to the Hallam Street flat to read the evening paper from cover to cover. Afterwards she could never look at the last pages of the *Evening Standard* without recovering that sense of utter desolation that had once driven her to read them rather than sit alone and think.

Usually, on her way home, she would stop at a snack-bar and buy a fish-cake or a sausage-roll that would serve for her supper. The tiny electric cooker in an alcove of the flat offered no scope for more elaborate cooking, nor had Deborah any heart for it. There was a restaurant in the block of flats and sometimes Deborah would take her newspaper and eat her supper there, but this she could not often afford to do; all her earnings were swallowed up by the rent she paid Madeleine and the weekly fare to Winchester ate largely into her private income.

The first weekend she went back she felt she could not bear to leave again. Already she saw Timmy a stranger, a strange child who had developed habits and pastimes unknown to her. She could not understand what compulsion had possessed her to leave him, what compulsion drove her away again. I've only got to get rid of Mrs Chalmers, she told herself, and the Ministry would have to release me, but somehow, each weekend she was in the train again on her way back to the lonely flat.

Madeleine at first was quite prepared to make Deborah's life less lonely. She accepted as a natural obligation that for a week or two she would introduce Deborah to people until gradually Deborah could build up a circle of her own. But Deborah resisted all Madeleine's suggestions for companionable evenings; if I once give in, she told herself, I'm done for, certain in her own mind that even a sherry-party or a game of bridge could have only one conclusion. She martyred herself till her very martyrdom became her excuse for her release.

For that first month she had accepted no mitigation of her lot. Once or twice she had been to the pictures with one or other of the girls from the office – but afterwards the bed sitting-room seemed only more lonely and more desolate. Once or twice Madeleine had had no one to go out with or to come and see her, and they sat by the fire and talked till Deborah was wild with envy of the glamour every word of Madeleine's life brought before her. But I'm being good for Graham, she would tell herself, and insensibly her grudge against him began to build itself up.

II

Madeleine had gone out on a wave of silver foxes and smuggled perfume and orchids. Deborah was sitting in front of her electric radiator trying to make the crossword puzzle last till it was time to open the baked beans and put them in the saucepan. The doorbell rang and she went to answer it.

An American officer was standing there. He was short and square, light-haired and smiling. He asked, 'Have I got to the right place? Is this Mrs Crayshaw's apartment?'

Deborah said, 'Yes, it is, but I'm afraid she's out. Was she expecting you?'

The officer looked disappointed. He said, 'Well, isn't that just too bad? No, she wasn't expecting me, but a friend of mine, William Selnick, told me to be sure and call on Mrs Crayshaw as soon as I got over. Maybe you've heard her speak of him.'

Deborah said kindly, 'Yes, I'm sure I have,' without bothering to think about it. She added politely, 'Have you just got to England?'

By this time he was in the hall and Deborah was leaning on the radiator. He offered her a cigarette and explained, 'Well, not exactly. But I've been in the West Country, training, for the past two months, and I've only just got posted to London. In fact, I've only just arrived and I don't know a soul.' He smiled at Deborah, and added, 'excepting you, of course. You'll be a friend of Mrs Crayshaw's?'

'I share the flat with her,' Deborah said. The conversation stopped. The officer showed no sign of going, and Deborah, suddenly remembering all she had read about American

hospitality, felt she must say, 'I'm sure Madeleine would never forgive me if I let any friend of William's go off without a drink. Won't you come in?'

He took off his trench coat, and said heartily, 'That's certainly very nice of you, Mrs — Mrs —?' He looked enquiringly at her wedding ring, and she said, 'I'm Mrs Robertson, Deborah Robertson. My husband's in the Middle East, so I'm doing a war job here in Town.'

He followed her into Madeleine's sitting-room and told her, 'I'm Joe Sadler from New York. My wife's back there right now. She was hoping to get sent over with the Red Cross, but she started a baby just before I was due to leave, so it looks like it'll be some time before I see her again.'

'That's too bad,' Deborah said, rummaging in the cupboard where Madeleine kept her drinks. She looked up and told him, 'There isn't an awful lot here. Would you like the dregs of a bottle of sherry or some gin and grapefruit?'

He looked over her shoulder and took hold of a bottle of whisky. 'This is what I like, if you can spare it,' he said. Deborah explained, 'This is Madeleine's drink, not mine. My room's next door, and I haven't any drink in it. But I'm sure she'd like you to have it. Help yourself.'

He picked up two glasses, and pouring the whisky out, said, 'Say when.'

Deborah shocked, exclaimed, 'Oh, I don't drink whisky, thanks. I'll just watch you.'

Joe Sadler said in concern, 'Listen, that's too bad. I can't drink all on my own. I wonder, Mrs Robertson, if you'd think me very impertinent if I made a suggestion?'

'No, I'm sure I wouldn't,' Deborah said slowly.

'Well, look here,' he said, 'if you're not all dated up for later on, I wonder if you'd give me the great privilege of taking you out to dinner. I can assure you you'd be doing a real kindness to a lonely stranger.'

'Listen, Mr Sadler,' Deborah said, 'no, it's Lieutenant, isn't it?'

'Lootenant,' he said, and grinned at her. 'But I hope it will soon be Joe.'

'Well anyway,' she persisted, 'I've got a husband in the Middle East and a baby in the country and I'm working because I want to get the war finished off for both their sakes. And that's the reason I'm in London, and that's the reason I'm used to being lonely in the evenings.'

He looked her firmly in the eyes. 'Mrs Robertson,' he said, 'you've answered me just as I'd want my wife to answer any impertinent stranger who had the gumph to ask her out on such short acquaintance. But – well, if he was really a nice guy and understood just how she was feeling, and was feeling rather the same himself, well, if he asked her again, I'd like her to accept instead of going on being lonely. Mrs Robertson, will you come and have dinner with me?'

'I'd love to,' said Deborah. She smiled brilliantly at him, and he thought how pretty she was with her long fair hair and her wide blue eyes. He asked, 'Has anyone ever told you you look rather like Veronica Lake?'

'No,' said Deborah, 'you're the first, Lootenant. Now if you wouldn't mind drinking whisky by yourself for a few minutes, I'll just go and put on something pretty for you.' She

went into her own room and hurriedly changed into a black afternoon frock, made up her face, and brushed her hair with brilliantine. I really must make an effort to get some perfume, she told herself, there's plenty floating around if you know where to pick it up; Mady's always got plenty. She hesitated a moment, then went into Madeleine's room, chose a bottle, and dabbed some about her, thinking how lucky she was to have come across this extraordinarily decent bloke with whom it was clearly quite all right to go out.

She went back into the sitting-room, and Joe Sadler said, 'Jeez, I certainly am going to be proud to be seen out with you. Now you'll have to tell me where to go, Mrs Robertson, for I haven't found my way around this town as yet.'

Deborah said tentatively, 'Do you think you'd like Quaglino's?' rather disliking the idea of going there again, yet preferring to take him to a place of which she had some knowledge.

He said heartily, 'Anywhere you say, Mrs Robertson,' and Deborah rang up and booked a table. 'I've made it for eight,' she said, 'in case we can't get a taxi, and have to walk all the way.'

'We'll get a taxi,' Joe said confidently, 'the Yanks always do,' and sure enough they picked one up as soon as they stepped into Hallam Street.

They sat and drank cocktails while they waited for their table. It was all so much like last time that Deborah constantly glanced round the room, half hoping, half fearing to see Peter again.

'Now, Mrs Robertson,' said Joe, 'I'm wanting to hear all

about that baby of yours. I'm getting to be mighty interested in babies.'

'He's rather a lamb,' Deborah said with a sigh, 'at least I think he is,' and in answer to Joe's questions she talked about Timmy till it was time to go in and have dinner, thinking how pleasantly different was this sane healthy conversation from the suggestion and innuendo that had been in every word she had exchanged with Peter.

Over dinner it was Joe's turn. He was a lawyer, he told her, and he'd married Marilyn just before Pearl Harbour, when it was clear that the States would be in sooner or later, 'and I kind of thought it would be sooner,' he said. Marilyn's parents were wealthy business people – he showed Deborah a snapshot of her standing beside an expensively groomed swimming pool at their place on Long Island. 'She's a lovely girl, isn't she?' he asked, and Deborah said enthusiastically yes, she was indeed a lovely girl, and so she was, as expensively groomed as the swimming pool and with, in addition, a kindly strength and honesty in her face. Joe, talking about the baby that was coming, discussed the names they might choose for it, and whether they could still fit in to the New York apartment or whether they'd have to change their whole way of life. Deborah got the impression of a moneyed background where nurses and maids were taken for granted, where rooms were furnished, clothes bought, entertainments arranged without regard for expense, and she accepted the champagne that Joe pressed on her and instinctively adapted her talk of her own background to bring it nearer the level on which she pictured Joe's.

It was ten o'clock, and Deborah said, 'I must be getting back. I'm a working girl and I've got to be up early.' This time they couldn't find a taxi and they walked home together in the dark, Joe holding Deborah's arm and pressing it close to his body.

But that was all. At the door of her flat, while she hesitated, he said, 'No, I'll not come in. But I certainly do want to thank you for the best evening I've had since I came to this country. Well, good night, Mrs Robertson, you'll be hearing from me,' and he was gone.

The next day, during her lunch hour, Deborah bought a hat. I've hardly, she said to herself, bought anything at all since the beginning of the war, and it does look rather poor to go round London like a country girl up for the day. So she spent a couple of weeks' salary on a hat that would never do for daytime wear at all and encouraged her to spend the afternoon mentally planning wardrobes that accorded in no way with either her income or her intended mode of life. It seemed to her, then, no more than she expected that when she got back to the flat there should be waiting for her a bunch of orchids, which she pinned to the black dress into which she changed.

At seven o'clock Joe was at her door. 'I certainly am glad to find you home,' he said, 'I've been kicking myself all day for forgetting to get your phone number, so's I could ask you if you'd honour me again tonight. Or are you all dated up?'

'You forget,' said Deborah sadly, 'that I told you I haven't been going places or wanting to. Only I usually slip on some-

thing pretty just to keep my morale up,' which was a lie as it was the first time she had done so.

Joe said, 'My morale needs keeping up too,' and Deborah was easily persuaded to put on her new hat and wish she had a coat to go with it and cling to Joe's arm as they went out into the black-out.

In the taxi she asked, 'Where are we going?'

'A guy at headquarters recommended the Lansdowne,' said Joe, 'so I booked a table on the chance you'd like it.'

Deborah did like it and they ate and drank and danced and talked seriously about marriage and women's attitude to men, and men's attitude to women. They found it extraordinary how similar were their ideas. A great many sentences began, 'what I don't like is when a husband – or a wife' – and each stored up the information gained about the imperfections in the other's private life. Still the discussion was overtly most impersonal, and the knowledge that the marital partner of neither could possibly object to such friendly comforting companionship was strongly in the minds of both. The next day was Friday, and Deborah, secure from a lonely Monday ahead, found she was enjoying her time with Timmy much more than usual, and decided that she had been leading an unhealthily secluded life for the past month and had been getting unnecessarily morbid as a result of it.

The next week she went out again with Joe, and again the week after. By this time, guys known to Joe had recommended him to most of the restaurants and night-clubs of London, Deborah had found it essential to buy a new frock, so as not always to appear in the same one, and they had

progressed to discussing sex with a quite impersonal fervour. This weekend before they parted, Joe had said, 'Listen, you come back Sunday evenings, don't you? What about my meeting your train and we'd go and eat some place?'

'Well, I don't usually get in till latish,' Deborah said, 'and I eat sandwiches on the train.'

'But that's no sort of a meal,' Joe expostulated. 'What time do you get to London?'

'Nine twenty-six,' said Deborah. 'If I leave any earlier I don't have time to see Timmy into bed, and honestly, I don't think we could find a meal at that time on a Sunday.'

He gloomily agreed. Deborah said suddenly, 'Suppose I bring something up with me and you come and have supper with me at the flat? Would that be a good idea?'

Joe said it would be perfectly swell. He added that he would provide the drink and would meet Deborah at Waterloo. So this weekend was enlivened for Deborah by the planning of a meal that would impress without grandeur.

III

The meal finally consisted of some fried sausages and chips and a tart made of some raspberries Deborah had bottled just after Graham went away. Joe said, 'This is much better than some stuffy nightclub,' and poured out a glass of whisky for Deborah to drink with her coffee. He said, 'For the first time since I left New York, I feel I'm in a home again,' and Deborah, sitting on the hearthrug at his feet felt, too, that nothing made one feel quite so normal and happy and

54

relaxed as a pleasantly cooked meal and a man in the house to share it with.

Inevitably that evening they made love to each other, though within very well defined limits. The next evening when Joe came round, Deborah said, 'Joe, it's no good, I don't think I ought to see you again. I've loved your friendship and all the times we've had together, but it's getting dangerous. I think we'd better say goodbye.'

Joe said, 'Darling, I was pretty sure you'd be feeling this way, and, knowing you, I understand just how you feel. But I want to have a talk with you and I can't talk on an empty stomach. I've got a table at the Apéritif where we can just talk quietly, and I want you to come.'

Put that way, of course, it would have been childish of Deborah to refuse. But she went hatless in her daytime tweed-suit to emphasise the moral distinction between this evening of formal discussion and those beglamoured ones that had gone before.

They chatted of quite impersonal things during dinner, except for the moment when Joe clutched at Deborah's hand and Deborah said, 'No!' and dragged it away with an agonised frustration on her face. But when the coffee and the Cointreau had been placed on the table, Joe said sternly, 'Now we've got to have this thing out.'

Deborah, looking down at her hands, said tonelessly, 'I don't think there's anything to have out. We like each other, and seeing so much of each other and both being lonely, well, I suppose something of the sort was bound to happen.'

Joe said deeply, 'There's more to it than that, isn't there?'

Deborah cried out, 'You love your wife, I love my husband. That's real. What happened to you and me is just wartime. We couldn't help getting too fond of each other, but we've got to stop before it goes any further. I don't want to let Graham down, and I'd be afraid to go on seeing you – now.'

'Do you think,' asked Joe, 'that you're seeing this thing quite straight?'

Deborah suddenly experienced that common sensation that all this had happened before, together with a complete foreknowledge of its development and ending. The sensation passed and with it some of her tenseness; she was conscious of pretence as she lifted her head and looked into Joe's eyes and then down at her hands again.

'Deborah,' said Joe, 'I want to tell you what my wife said to me in New York just before I came away. She said, "Joe, you're a normal man and we're maybe going to be parted for a long time. It's no good shutting our eyes to what's likely to happen, but I'm going to ask you one thing. Don't cheapen our marriage. I'd hate to think of you going with any cheap woman and then coming back to me. But if you ever find a girl you can really respect, like you do me, I wouldn't mind so much, because it wouldn't be cheap."'

Deborah remembered Graham promising her that he'd only sleep with cheap women because anything else would encroach on his relationship with her. It doesn't seem to matter what you promise, she thought, so long as you promise something.

Joe was still talking. 'Well,' he said, 'I made her that promise and I intend to stick to it, no matter what. I thought

it would be difficult to keep because I didn't see myself finding another woman I could respect like I do my wife. But I have. You know the way I feel about you, Deborah. Won't you let us both be happy together?'

Deborah lifted her head. 'Joe,' she said, 'I can't pretend after last night that you don't mean anything to me, because you know you do. But I love my husband and my baby, and I'm not going to do anything that would let them down.'

'Listen,' said Joe earnestly, 'I respect your feelings and I can understand them. But you've got to take the long view. Your husband may be away for years. It's not good for a woman to live without a man for years. I'd be willing to bet that already you get all on edge sometimes so you don't know what to do with yourself. Well, that may be conventional morality, but it's not giving that boy of yours the calm and happy sort of mother he's got a right to, particularly with his father away.'

Deborah gave a strained laugh and said, 'You can't be asking me to go to bed with you for my baby's sake. How would you feel if your own wife did the same?'

'I'd want her to,' Joe said, 'I'd want her to do anything that would keep her the normal and happy woman I'd left, and not have her all frustrated and then having a grudge against me for causing it. Look here, when you're feeling that way, don't you often get to almost hating your husband and blaming him for being away?'

'Yes,' said Deborah slowly, 'I do.'

Joe urged, 'I don't know about *your* husband, but I'd certainly hate to have my wife feeling that way about me. I'd sooner have her do anything than take to blaming me and

building up a grudge against me for something that wasn't my fault.'

Deborah said nothing. The argument was now completely satisfying and unanswerable. Something more was needed. Joe took her hand and held it between his.

'Darling,' he said, 'please let us enjoy each other. I want you so badly and I'm so fond of you. I know I can make you happy if you'll let me.'

Deborah moved her hand caressingly in his and gave a quick little nod of her head. Joe said, 'Oh, darling, you're so wonderful,' and Deborah turned on him a shy confiding stare. She whispered, 'You'll be kind to me, won't you?' and Joe said, 'Darling, you know I will, there's nothing I won't do to keep you happy.' He squeezed her hand and said, 'Let's get out of here.' They went back to the flat, and Joe spent the night with Deborah, sidling out furtively in the morning so that Madeleine should not know.

CHAPTER FOUR

All that day Deborah felt well and proud and happy. Not only that, she felt brave and self-confident. I know I've done the right thing, she said, at any rate it's the right thing for me though it might not be for everybody. Now I can think of Graham with all the love I really have for him, and she thought of Graham hard and conscientiously, without noticing the new note of contemptuous pity that had now slid into her love for him, the inevitable pity and contempt of a woman for her cuckolded husband.

When she got back to the flat that evening she found a letter from him that Mrs Chalmers had forwarded from the cottage. It was the first she had received since she had written to tell him she was going to London.

Deborah darling, he wrote, letters take such an appalling time to get here that by the time you get this, it will be quite out of date. But I can't help saying that I personally would have been happier to think of you and Timmy safely together in the cottage, particularly in view of bombs. Still, you're on the spot and you've got to decide, and I quite understand that you might find life easier with a full-time job to keep you

occupied. Incidentally, couldn't you have found one in Winchester? I must admit I'm a bit worried about the financial aspect of it all, though I suppose you've got all that well in hand. You haven't given me the address of the friend you're sharing with and I hope it isn't Madeleine. I know we have her to thank for our first meeting, but I still wouldn't like to think of you living with her. This sounds a horribly carping sort of letter, but you did ask for my advice, and it's fiendishly difficult to give it from such a distance in time and geography. Anyway, what I really want is that you should be happy and contented, and go on remembering how much I love you.

Criticism from people whose admiration she sought always tore Deborah to pieces. I wish I'd had this yesterday, she thought, it might have made a difference, but now everything is changed and it's too late anyway. She knew she should sit down now and answer this letter, give Graham some assurance, but there was none she could honestly give him without pulling down the edifice of the new life she had so laboriously justified for herself. I'll answer it at the weekend, she decided, I feel more in sympathy with Graham at the cottage than I do here, and she bathed and changed and got herself ready for Joe.

Eventually she wrote to Graham.

Darling, your letter upset me a little, because I got the impression you're worried about me, and you've really got no cause to be. All this talk you hear about air-raids

in London is very much exaggerated, there's hardly anything going on now, and as for cash, my earnings more than cover my expenses here. I did try first of all to get a job in Winchester, but I couldn't find anything really interesting and worthwhile, which it had to be if it was worth doing at all. Do go on writing to the cottage, because though I'm at the moment sharing a flat with a girl from the office, it may be only a temporary arrangement and I'd hate to have your letters go astray, while the cottage will always find me. Timmy is quite adorable now, I do so wish you were here to see him . . .

II

Very quickly Deborah's life with Joe achieved a recognisable pattern. Now that she was definitely his mistress, she had a relationship with him that was accepted by his friends as formal and permanent within the limits imposed by war. Now he would bring his friends home to drink at the flat, now he would take her out to dine with his friends and their mistresses, so that the regular tempo of a married life imposed itself upon them. Very soon, the situation was admitted to Madeleine and accepted by her, so that the social life inside the flat became more communal and general. Once the fundamental fact was accepted that all the relationships within this circle were extra-marital ones, the social life they entailed was as conventionally ordinary as the social life of ordinary married couples. It was inevitably less permanent.

Periodically the men in the circle would disappear; a wife would come over from the States, a wife would have a baby, a man might be sent overseas, or he might change his mistress. But though a woman in the circle might change her lover, she seldom left it to return to the demands of conventional life.

Deborah enjoyed to the full the enormously enhanced financial level on which she was now living. Practically all the men among whom she moved were American officers with, by English standards, enormous salaries and nothing to spend them on but personal enjoyment. When she would, with Graham, have thought that an evening at the theatre followed by a dinner in Soho a rare celebration and treat, an average evening with Joe would include drinks at the popular bar of the moment, dinner and dancing at the most expensive level, and a night-club to follow. Where, with Graham, Deborah had always said primly, 'Three drinks an evening is my limit,' with Joe she soon stopped counting her drinks at all, and took as normal the state of at least slight intoxication in which every evening with him was passed.

The other women in the circle were very like Deborah herself; most of them were married and separated from their husbands either by some incompatibility or an accident of war. They came from roughly the same social level as herself, but she was the newest and least experienced of them all. She never met them except in the company of their men, and the only private conversations she had with them were in ladies' cloakrooms where they almost invariably discussed illicit methods of acquiring silk stockings. To be able to do this was a social indispensability; methods varied from the use

of the diplomatic bags of various South American republics to knowing a ferry pilot, although to receive them from a husband overseas, as Deborah did, was by far the most usual.

Insensibly Deborah's own standard of living crept up. So many things became necessities that had been unnecessary before – bottles of sherry and nail-varnish and perfumes and hair-do's. At last she decided that it would be no more than sensible to draw some money out of the Post Office and get some new clothes more suited to her present life than those she owned already.

Deborah had already passed through three distinct phases of dressing. In the first, in Leeds, she had been dressed by her mother in expensive styleless clothes that lasted for years and were good by no standard but that of quality. In the second, at the Slade, she had reacted against this to bright colours and picturesque cut, dramatic effects and fantastic old jewellery. After she married she had worn not very good tweeds with nice pullovers and rather showy flat shoes. But now she yearned for sophistication, for sleek black frocks, and, more than anything else, for an immense variety of expensively nonsensical hats.

III

She said to Joe, 'I'm going to buy a hat in my lunch-hour tomorrow. Want to come and help me choose it?'

'I'm rather good at choosing hats,' Joe said, and they went together to the extremely expensive hatshop recommended by Madeleine where all the hats were suitable for dining in restaurants and none of them for going to church in the country.

The saleswoman automatically deferred to Joe and so did Deborah, both of them half-playing at submission to his fancy, each rigidly determined, the one to sell, the other to buy her specific choice.

At last, the decision was between two hats, both enchanting, glamorous, outrageously costly. 'I just can't decide,' said Deborah. 'They're both utterly adorable and I really can't run to more than one of them.'

'Suppose you let me give you the other?' suggested Joe.

The sales-lady meditatively stroked the hat she was holding on her hand.

Deborah said, 'Don't be silly,' and then to the saleswoman, 'I think I'd just like to try the other on again before I decide.'

'But you don't have to decide,' said Joe. 'I'm giving you the other.'

For a moment Deborah's resolution hung suspended. There were two courses of action, each reasonable, each convincing. She took off the hat she was wearing and laid it on the table before her. She said to the sales-woman in a detached voice, 'I really can't make up my mind now. I'll think it over and come back tomorrow.'

Joe said earnestly, 'Darling –' but Deborah picked up her bag and gloves and Joe had to follow her.

They walked silently side by side under the arcades of the Ritz, along Piccadilly, into Green Park. Deborah sat down on a bench and Joe sat down beside her. She stared straight in front of her, deliberately ignoring him, and he asked, 'What's the matter?'

Deborah still stared stiffly in front of her. She said coldly, 'If you really don't know what's the matter, that seems to me to make the whole situation infinitely worse.'

In sincere perplexity Joe said, 'Honest, I don't know what this is all about. I can't see I've done anything to get you like this.'

Now Deborah turned on him, her eyes lustrous with angry tears. 'I've been kidding myself,' she said swiftly, 'I'd thought that we were really fond of each other, that we'd got something that was decent and true. It was on my side. I was just a fool, that's all. I hadn't realised you were just looking on me as a cheap common tart.'

'But, darling,' said Joe, bewildered, 'what can have made you think that? It just doesn't begin to be true.'

Without listening to him, Deborah went on, 'I could have stood it all if you hadn't insulted me in front of that bloody woman in the shop. Now I'll never be able to go there again and I don't know anywhere else to go.'

'I'd like to know,' Joe said, 'just what I did that was so insulting.'

'Well,' cried Deborah wildly, 'I'm sorry if you can't see it's insulting to come with me to buy a hat and then offer to pay for it, just as if I was a kept woman. All your talk about respecting me like you do your wife is just so much hot air. I'm just your mistress, that's all, and it doesn't matter if all the shops in London know it. But I wish I'd realised it myself instead of believing you when you said you thought of me differently.'

Joe had a momentary impulse to lose his temper and say, So what, you are my mistress, so what's biting you? But he was shocked at himself finding the convention of mutual respect as necessary as Deborah did, and so he said instead, 'Darling, you've got the whole thing absolutely wrong. Suppose you wipe your eyes and relax a bit, and I'll tell you what really happened?'

Deborah said coldly, 'I'd simply adore to know,' but when Joe took hold of her hand, she let it lie in his, limp and unresisting.

'You see,' Joe began, 'when I was back home in New York, I used to go shopping with my wife, just like I did with you today. It got to be a sort of joke between us, that she'd buy what she wanted with her own money, and then I'd throw in something extra on top. So when you took me along with you today, well, the last thing I was doing was thinking of you as my mistress. I was acting just like I did back home with my wife.'

He squeezed her hand and her fingers gave a faint responsive flutter then hung limp again.

Joe urged, 'You do understand now, don't you, darling? It's all OK again?'

Deborah stood up and said in a faint weak voice, 'I must go back to work now, I'll be late.' He walked beside her, and as they went she said, looking away from him, 'I suppose I haven't got the right to make a fuss about a thing like that. It's just that it seemed quite unendurable to be put publicly in that sort of position.'

He squeezed her elbow sympathetically and they walked on silently. At the entrance to the Ministry, Joe said, 'I'll be

along the usual time,' and Deborah smiled sadly and made no answer.

IV

As she was dressing that evening Deborah thought angrily, I wish I'd slipped out at tea-time and bought one of the hats, knowing instinctively that after such a scene it was wiser to appear as different, as newly glamorous as possible. In lieu of this, she made her eyes up more heavily than usual so that she looked satisfyingly sophisticated and incapable of emotion.

The doorbell rang and she went to answer it. Joe was carrying a parcel that clearly contained a hat. Deborah immediately averted her eyes from this and made no comment when he laid it on the hall floor and came into her sitting-room.

She had mixed two cocktails and now handed him one with a consciously careless and attractive smile. But Joe put his carefully on the table and moved towards her.

'Deborah,' he said with great solemnity, 'I haven't been able to stop thinking about what you said to me today. I just can't stand you believing that I'm not respecting you like you'd wish. But we've got to get things straight. When a man loves a girl, it's his natural instinct to want to give her things. It's not like it is with a woman who's just a kept woman; then you've got to give her things for payment. But it's not like that with us. I've been trying all afternoon to find a way to make you understand that, and at last I thought of this way. It's just up to you whether you understand or not.'

He put his hand in his pocket and pulled out a little parcel. Deborah took it and undid it to reveal a jeweller's box. Inside it was a pair of exquisite Victorian garnet earrings.

She looked at the earrings and then questioningly at Joe.

He said heavily, 'I gave my wife a pair of old earrings like those when we first got engaged. I wouldn't have thought then that I'd ever have wanted to give another woman a present that meant so much in my life, but I know this is the proper present for you. Will you accept it with my love and understand how I mean it for a symbol of what we mean to each other?'

Deborah said with a sob, 'Oh, Joe,' and flung her arms round his neck. She thought, as she sobbed on his shoulder, they're absolutely gorgeous earrings, but I'll have to go and change my lipstick; I don't think I've got one quite dark enough.

Joe gently disengaged her arms and said, 'Drink up your cocktail.' And as Deborah obediently and happily drank, he added, 'And to show you I'm not standing any nonsense from you, I've bought you both those hats and I want to see you wearing them. I'm going to buy my girl just what I please, from now on.'

V

And so he did. Deborah rapidly acquired those appurtenances that were recognised in her circle as being of almost as great importance as caste marks; it was essential that a woman should have a slim gold lighter and a jewel-encrusted gold powder-compact; that she should have smuggled perfumes and lipsticks and other fards from countries that did not take the conception of war as austerely as England. But with the acceptance of these presents, Deborah and Joe found it necessary to affirm the special character of their relationship rather more frequently; neither would have had any defences left if it had become accepted as simply that of a lover with his mistress.

One topic that they found invariably gave their conversations an odour of respectability was that of Deborah's little son. Joe was, in fact, far more genuinely homesick than he could have possibly believed, and really found solace in talking of the baby Deborah had got and thinking of the baby he was soon to have.

So at last he said, 'Darling, aren't you ever going to let me become really acquainted with your son? What do you say we bring him up to town one Saturday and take him round the Zoo?'

Deborah, unworried by air-raids for herself, had an unreasoning dread of them for Timmy. Much more than Joe's suggestion would have been needed before she would consent to a day of agony of pictorial imagination, during which she would be haunted by visions of Timmy torn by shrapnel, Timmy crushed by falling houses, Timmy dying alone in the dark and believing himself deserted. She said, 'I think it would be a much better idea if you came and spent a weekend with us at the cottage. The blossom is just beginning to come out and it ought to be rather lovely.'

'That'd be swell,' Joe said heartily, 'how about next weekend? I could come down with you on the Friday evening.'

'We'd have to make up a story for Mrs Chalmers,' Deborah said quickly. 'I don't think it would be quite the thing for me to bring a boyfriend down. You've no idea how people talk in English villages.'

'I sure have,' Joe agreed heartily, 'that's to say if they're anything like our villages back home. Still, we can fix up a yarn. How'd it be if I said I was a friend of your husband's?'

'He's never been to the States,' Deborah temporised. She felt a strong repugnance to bringing her husband and Joe into even a putative relationship. 'You might have known his parents – they've been in the States all the war.'

'Say, that's a bit complicated,' Joe protested. 'I might get myself all tied up. Don't you think it would be better if we said that they'd asked some pal of mine to look you up, and as he couldn't make it, I'd come instead?'

'That will do beautifully,' agreed Deborah, and rang up Mrs Chalmers to tell her of the weekend guest.

VI

Joe picked Deborah up at the office that Friday with a large knobbly brown-paper parcel. 'I got him a wooden train,' he explained to Deborah, 'it's not as nice as I'd have liked, but I wanted to take the kid something.'

Deborah was pleased and appreciative. If, she felt, this bringing together of her son and her lover could be successful, then it might bring some satisfactory synthesis in her own life; now she lived two separate ones and was not wholly happy in either.

Timmy, was, of course, in bed when they arrived, but Deborah, tiptoeing and with her finger on her lips, took Joe up to see him in his cot. The child lay there, sleep-flushed, his fair curls damp on his head, his thumb stuck firmly into his mouth. Deborah looked at him and some intensity of emotion, of deep pity, made her eyes fill with tears. Joe suddenly gripped her hand and said in a hoarse voice, 'He should have been ours.'

Deborah was momentarily and instinctively repelled. Then habit reasserted itself and she pressed his hand with unspoken acquiescence in his outburst. They went downstairs where Mrs Chalmers had laid herself out to produce an especially good meal and was more than ready to like Joe for his effusive praise of it.

After the meal, Mrs Chalmers disappeared to wash up and Deborah and Joe sat in armchairs and drank their coffee. Both felt a relaxation they had not known before together, and for a while neither spoke. At last Joe said in a half whisper, 'Darling, don't you wish this was all real?'

'How do you mean?' Deborah said, rather unwilling to understand.

'We met too late,' Joe said, staring into the fire, 'This should all have been ours together, a home, a baby that belonged to us both. Darling, don't you feel it too?'

Deborah was frightened and yet glad. Here was the ultimate reassurance she had always wanted from Joe, yet now it seemed threatening, potentially dangerous. But she was incapable of withdrawing from melodrama and so she said in an expressionless voice, 'It's too late now.'

Joe lifted his head, and said, 'Is it?' He made a movement towards her and Deborah said nervously, 'Hush,' as she heard Mrs Chalmers' footsteps nearing the door.

At half-past ten, Mrs Chalmers rolled up her knitting and said she supposed it was time for beddy-byes. She looked enquiringly at Deborah who said with an attempt at natural-ness, 'I'm just going to listen to some dance music for a bit. Somehow I don't feel tired enough to go to bed yet.' Joe stood up and opened the door for Mrs Chalmers, who hesitated and then went heavily upstairs.

Joe said, 'Let's have some of these lights off and be cosy.' He switched on the radio, and gradually drugged by the jazz Joe and Deborah lay in each other's arms in one of the big armchairs and made love.

At eleven, their love-making was chilled by the astringent news. Joe said, 'Oh, damn,' and got up to switch the radio off. Deborah stood up and tidied her hair. She said, 'I suppose we ought to go to bed now,' and Joe came back to her, and said hoarsely, 'Darling, can I come to your room for a few minutes? I must.'

Again his importunity repelled her. She thought con-fusedly, no, it's not right, this is my husband's house, Timmy's here, it's indecent. But no idea of putting these thoughts into words crossed her mind; instead, she said, 'Darling, I'd love it, but it's quite impossible. That woman's got ears like a cat, we'll have to wait,' and then softly and with a simulacrum of intense desire, 'how much I wish we could.'

VII

Breakfast the next day was an uncomfortable meal. Deborah had become obsessed with the idea that Mrs Chalmers was suspicious of her relationship with Joe, and told too many unconvincing lies to show how formal and slight that relationship was. She need not have troubled; Mrs Chalmers did not notice that Deborah had no need to ask Joe how he liked his coffee and was wholly absorbed in the effect her Timmy was making on this amiable American who seemed so much to like her cooking and the homely atmosphere of the house.

But Timmy at breakfast was an awkward burden to all of them. Each vied with the other to make the child and his special relationship to that one the centre of attention, but Timmy was coy and uneasy, sensing some new threat to his constantly altering security. He had had to adjust himself too much already to emotional change and loss, and his main distrust was of Deborah, of whom he had the greatest need. So he shamed her before Joe by shaking himself free from her embraces, turning whining to Mrs Chalmers for reassurance when Deborah gave him an order, ignoring the accepted breakfast routine that had been one of the staples of his life.

Mrs Chalmers said with an apologetic titter, 'Timmy's so over-excited at seeing you again, Mrs Robertson, he just doesn't know what to do with himself.' Deborah, loathing the imputation that she was a visitor in her son's life, still had to accept this with a smile, hoping that it would serve to excuse Timmy's behaviour to Joe.

After breakfast, Mrs Chalmers carried Timmy off upstairs and Deborah, dropping her cigarette into her coffee cup, said, 'What would you like to do now?'

Joe said politely, 'What do you usually do?'

Deborah replied vaguely, 'Oh, just drift about. Sometimes we play in the garden or sometimes I take Timmy for a walk and we drop in on people or something like that.'

'Well, I'd like to do that with you,' Joe said, 'I haven't seen any English villages in this part of the country.'

Deborah was a little uneasy. She had pictured the week-end playing with Timmy in the garden while Joe looked benignly and paternally on, not an excursion through the village with an American officer that might tend to dissipate the picture she wanted the village to hold of gallant lonely little Mrs Robertson working, oh, so hard up in London to bring her husband back the sooner. If Joe wants to walk round the village, she said to herself, we'll simply have to take Timmy too, even though he'll be a drag.

The walk was not enjoyed by either Deborah or Timmy. Timmy, finding most of his comments and pleas went unheard by the grown-ups, was reduced to whining and hanging on to his mother's hand. Deborah, anxious simultaneously to amuse and interest Joe, yet to do so with an appearance of detachment that might seem convincing to any of her acquaintances they met, could spare no time to amuse and interest Timmy and was angry with herself and with Joe for preventing it. As twelve o'clock struck, Joe said, 'Couldn't we go to the pub now and get a drink?' and Deborah, unable to resolve this awkward situation, willingly eliminated it by taking the miserable Timmy back to Mrs Chalmers.

Joe said heartily over their drinks that Timmy was a fine little chap and all kids were shy at first but Timmy would soon get over that when they knew each other better. Deborah, smiling acquiescence, discovered that the last thing on earth she wanted was a better acquaintance between the two and, simultaneously, that Americans tended to be crude and unperceptive. But there was still a day and a half of this weekend to get through, and she wondered how she could possibly arrange it that she had at least part of the time alone with Timmy to reassure him that his jealousy was unfounded and her allegiance to him undivided. In the end this proved impossible, as Joe understood the duties of a guest as entailing constant attendance on all activities of mother and son. And again Deborah, unable to achieve a satisfactory synthesis of the situation, escaped from it by accepting Joe's suggestion that they should leave earlier than usual on the Sunday so as to be sure of getting a table at the Savoy.

VIII

Next day at the office, Deborah wrote to Graham,

Darling, I can't stand it any longer, honestly I can't. I've tried and tried, and I just miss you so desperately that life doesn't seem to have any meaning now. It's not fair, the way war means that women have got to be left alone with all their lives pulled to pieces. It's all right for men, they've got things to do and friends, they don't get time for being alone and miserable. But I just

can't stand it any more. I know I ought to be brave and take it on the chin and all that, but I just can't. I don't know what I'll do.

Graham wrote to this a loving answer, entreating his wife to have courage and patience and offering her all the comfort a letter could give. But before his answer reached her, before her first letter had arrived, Deborah had dashed off another note to him, saying that the first was a reflection of a passing mood, and, though she was sorry to have inflicted this mood on him, the fact that she felt free to do so should be taken as a measure of her love and of her confidence in his.

For Deborah's temporary distaste for Joe in rural surroundings passed quickly when they were back in London together. A new relationship developed between them after that weekend and it was one that Deborah found in every way satisfactory. Now Joe was avowedly in love with Deborah, desirous constantly of telling her how much he wished that circumstances could allow of them making a permanent life together; while Deborah, now despising Joe for her too easy mastery of him, eased her conscience to the utmost by equally constantly reminding Joe of his former love for his wife and his future duty to her. It was never admitted by Deborah that had it not been for the calls of duty she could have wished nothing better than a future with Joe; still, she never denied it, and she allowed Joe to believe that this was her wish too.

Such a relationship was, however, incapable of indefinite duration, and it was a relief to Deborah when early that summer Joe had to tell her that he was being suddenly sent

abroad to an unknown destination. Their parting, naturally, was at a high emotional pitch. They had a final dinner together at L'Apéritif – both felt that dancing would have been altogether too frivolous in tone but they drank champagne as a gesture of reminiscence.

Joe put his hand over Deborah's. 'I can't help feeling,' he said earnestly, 'that maybe I've done you a great wrong. When I first met you you were all set just to do your job and wait for your husband to come back. Well, you know what happened. At the time it seemed good sense, but now I'm wondering if I wouldn't have done better by you if I hadn't persuaded you into this.'

The picture he presented was not altogether pleasing. Whenever Deborah was persuaded to do anything she wanted to do, she persuaded herself simultaneously that her change of intention was due to uninfluenced new conviction. This open assumption of persuasion suggested intolerable weakness.

Joe felt her change of mood and his hand tightened on hers. He said, 'Darling, it's only that I'm so afraid you may find it difficult to do without all this now.' He looked largely round the restaurant and added, 'God knows I hate to think of you sitting lonely in your flat like you did when I first found you, but I'd hate to have started something that might mess things up for you.'

Deborah said coldly, 'Do you mean you think you're likely to be the first of a series of affairs – or perhaps you don't think you were the first?'

Joe was shocked. He begged, 'I just hate to hear you talking like that. That's just the sort of thing I'm afraid of, that

I'm going to leave you even more hurt and miserable than you were before. Jeez, I don't know what I want for you, but I sure would hate to have started anything that spoilt things with your husband and that nice kid of yours.'

'Believe me,' said Deborah, 'I think quite as seriously of Graham and Timmy as you possibly could.'

'That's what I mean,' Joe said eagerly, 'but you've been getting me all wrong. What I said to you when we first met is still quite true. It isn't any good for you just to sit at home and mope, but surely there's girls you could go out and have a bit of a gay time with, girls from the office or old college friends or something. Darling, I'm not wanting you not to go out with other men because I'm going to be jealous, but for your own sake. You're so sweet and nice, I don't see how any guy could help falling for you and I want to think of you being happy without your having to wonder all the time whether you ought to be saying yes or no.'

'It's not going to be easy,' Deborah said, staring straight in front of her, 'you've taught me a lot of things, Joe. I liked them at the time, but I'm not sure I won't be sorry I learnt to do so. But I want to live decently – I know that sounds priggish,' she broke off, and looked appealingly at Joe. 'But I'll honestly try to have the sort of good time you mean. I'll have to have some sort of a good time, or I'll go crazy missing you.'

She was sincere because Joe had frightened her. She had had a vision of herself passing from man to man, passing ever more shoddily from the wife of Graham and the mother of Timmy.

'There's one more thing,' Joe said, 'I don't like to say this, but I feel I ought to. Deborah, I think you ought to consider living some place else. Madeleine's a nice girl all right when you're in that sort of a mood, but she's not the sort of girl I like to think of you living with. There's another thing about that – any guy who saw you going about with Madeleine would be apt to get the wrong ideas about the kind of girl you are.'

Graham had often said the same thing, but it was only after hearing it from Joe that Deborah, with a sudden shock, believed it. She said truthfully, 'I haven't thought of it that way,' and Joe said quickly, 'I know you hadn't, darling, you're much too nice, but you don't want someone else to go thinking it for you.' Deborah, terrified by this picture of false impressions now thrust upon her, threw Madeleine to the winds and said recklessly, 'God, I'll get out just as soon as I can. I just hadn't thought . . .'

CHAPTER FIVE

❦❦❦❦❦

Joe went abroad, and Deborah began trying to carry out the promises she had made him. Without saying anything to Madeleine, she asked several girls at the office to let her know if they heard of a suitable flat. No one was very hopeful about the possibility of finding one, which was a certain relief to Deborah who, while she stayed with Madeleine, could be sure of remaining at least in touch with contemporary glamour. Still, though the glamour was in no way diminished, she now had a certain fear of it, and kept up her enquiries for new flats she might live in.

She tried, too, to make a social life for herself with other women. This course was fraught with difficulties. In the first place, the attractive sophisticated girls, whom Deborah naturally preferred, were seldom in a phase of wanting to go out with other women too. To go out with the other girls from the office meant, as a gesture of dissipation, a theatre followed by a dinner in Soho, or, more usually, a film, and something after a queue at Lyons. Deborah's tarty hats lay limply in her wardrobe while she conscientiously and genuinely attempted to enjoy this form of social life, but still she felt that sitting at home alone with the evening papers and her loneliness

and her dreams held more excitement than this drab second-best.

But she went on trying. She hunted through telephone directories, questioned directory-enquiries and eventually found two former Slade friends who were still living near. She went to see them both. One was politically conscious, patently despised this new Deborah of smart clothes and glittering standards and showed no wish further to resume the acquaintance. The second, married, was living with her husband and babies in an outer suburb. Deborah went there to supper one evening and returned home depressed beyond measure by the sight of happy wedded life.

She said so to Madeleine into whose bedroom she wandered after she got back. Madeleine, intently plucking a recalcitrant hair from an eyebrow, said firmly, 'It's no good, darling, I tried it myself once. Once you're married and haven't got a husband, the only women you can go about with are other women who are in the same boat.'

'Why?' asked Deborah, sitting on the floor, pulling at a white fur rug.

Madeleine began patting cream into her neck. She said, 'It's obvious, once you come to think about it. A married woman is an experienced woman and men like experienced women. A husband who isn't there is just an invitation to some other man to fill his place. At the same time, the knowledge that you've got a husband makes another man feel safe; he doesn't feel you're in a position to tie him up, as you might be if you were unmarried or a widow.'

Deborah said, 'Yes, I can see that's all probably true, but

I'm not talking about getting off with men, I'm talking about getting on with women.'

'You can't separate the two,' Madeleine said simply, 'After all, all women want men, don't they, and women like us have got a hell of an advantage over all the others. If you go out with an unmarried girl and a man appears on the scene you've got him every time before she's even started and she knows it; what man is going to start an affair that may involve all sorts of responsibilities when he can have one without? In the same way, if you try to get on with married women with their husbands about them, sooner or later they're going to get worried. They're going to wonder how soon their husband is going to notice you and they're quite right, because sooner or later he always does. No husband can ever look at an attractive woman who hasn't got one, without thinking she's fair game and a damn good opportunity at that.'

'If that's really true,' Deborah said hopefully, 'it's no good my going on trying.'

Madeleine gave her a sideways glance. She said slowly, almost against her will, 'Deborah, why don't you go home? If all I've said *is* true, and I firmly believe it is, can't you see where it's going to lead you? It doesn't matter a damn to me, Edward and I are all washed up anyway, and I've only got myself to please. But you, surely, want to go back and live with your husband when the war's over and you've got a baby to keep you company while you wait for him. Just between you and me, you're damn lucky. Don't you think you'd be wiser to go home now rather than to risk spoiling it?'

This was so unpalatable to Deborah that she preferred to believe that Madeleine was insincere and had only her own ends in view. She's afraid of competition if I stayed around and she wants to see me out of the way, she decided happily; I'd certainly better go ahead with finding a flat of my own. The only effect Madeleine's words had was to open a vista of opportunity, and the suggestion that Deborah should withhold herself from such opportunities made them the more tantalising. So she said, as if ignoring Madeleine's last remark, 'Anyway, I've fixed up to go to a flick with a girl from the office tomorrow. If that isn't productive, I'll have to think again,' and went to bed, leaving Madeleine to wonder satirically just how productive a cinema with another woman could possibly be.

II

Actually the products of this particular excursion exceeded either Deborah's or Madeleine's expectations. For, as Deborah and her friend Christine were crossing the plush carpet of the foyer, a short dark American officer came over to Christine and said, 'Well, now, don't say you can't remember who I am?'

Christine, who was a nice timorous girl with a fiancé in the Ack-Ack, retreated a step and dithered. The American looked quickly and appreciatively at Deborah and pursued his efforts at recognition.

'We danced together at a hospital dance at Godalming,' he said to Christine, 'Sheldon Z. Wynuck is the name, and I remember you were wearing a very pretty green frock.'

At the mention of Godalming, Christine relaxed. Nothing wrong could have happened near her home town, where, if she had gone to a hospital dance, it would have been under the auspices of her mother. The only thing was, she was a little near-sighted and never found it easy, in any case, to distinguish one American from another. So she said politely, 'I believe I do remember. How nice to see you again,' and then searching for something to say, 'Have you seen the film, or were you just going in?'

'Just going in,' said Sheldon Z. Wynuck, with another quick look, almost a wink at Deborah, 'I'm hoping you ladies will be good enough to let me escort you,' and he took them each by the arm and they went to their seats together.

Deborah sat limply in her seat with a sensation of inevitability. She had said that this evening must produce something – and it had. She glanced at Sheldon Z. Yes, he was a lieutenant – like Joe. He was an American – like Joe. She accepted him as a gift from fate, and his superficial community with Joe made it then possible for her to transfer to him all the defensive arguments that in the case of Joe had been so potent. More than that, by equating the appearance of Sheldon with the working of fate, she felt she had a certain responsibility to fulfil its machinations, so that when, in the darkness, Sheldon's hand reached out and clasped hers, she did not feel it necessary to make any gesture of withdrawal.

It must be remembered that Sheldon had no sense of the workings of fate at all.

As they pushed out of the cinema Sheldon said, 'Let's go some place and have a cup of coffee.' This was a simple form

of pleasure that Joe and Deborah had somehow never indulged in, and believing therefore that Sheldon was as conscious of its simplicity as she was, she persuaded Christine that it would do no harm to squeeze their way into the crowded American snack-bar where Sheldon led them and was able to drink her cup of coffee with well-conditioned enjoyment.

Afterwards, on the pavement, Sheldon said, 'Now if I can only get hold of a taxi I hope you girls are going to let me take you home.' He looked from one to the other and Deborah let Christine protest, 'Oh, no, I couldn't possibly, I get the tube direct from here anyway,' and said good night to her and watched her walk away. Sheldon, with that instinctual dexterity that seems racial, procured a taxi and drove Deborah home.

Nothing was said between them. Sheldon paid off the taxi and followed Deborah into the flat and into her room. But it must still be remembered that Sheldon had no ideas about the workings of fate.

III

Consequently, the affair, from Deborah's point of view, soon showed itself wholly unsatisfactory. Her real trouble was simply that Sheldon wasn't Joe, and every time a difference in him made this manifest, Deborah resented it. Sheldon's attitude was far simpler; he had found a nice easy girl, just like he always found a nice easy girl, with the advantage that this one was rather tonier than any he'd had before. He did his best to repay her according to his usages, but his standards

just weren't Joe's. His knowledge of London restaurants and dance places for instance, was on an altogether lower social plane, and Deborah had always found the second-best particularly galling. Besides, when she passed Madeleine casually in the flat and Madeleine remarked, 'We had a good party at the Mirabelle last night,' it was galling to keep her mouth shut or admit that she and Sheldon merely sat and drank in the Piccadilly Brasserie.

Nor was Deborah for long conscious of the fact that the fine moral arguments that had persuaded her into bed with Joe no longer held validity when it so soon became clear that Sheldon had no notion that moral arguments even began to be appropriate to the situation. Sheldon began to jar on Deborah very much indeed and she might have got rid of him had there been the slightest prospect of being able to fill his place.

She tried to conceal Sheldon from Madeleine, referring to him lightly as 'my new Yank'. But a deep and burning jealousy of Madeleine grew up inside her, for Madeleine seemed to her to be possessed of a capacity that she, Deborah, entirely lacked and that was the capacity to attract what Deborah privately thought of as 'grown-ups'. Madeleine's conversation made it quite clear to Deborah that 'grown-ups' were the only sort of men that Madeleine bothered to like, and apparently she never had the slightest difficulty in attracting these, whether they were business men, full Colonels or, as she had recently confided to Deborah, 'the most marvellous Frenchman – about forty-five and something rather special.' Deborah, looking from Graham through Peter on to Sheldon and Joe, realised that none of these would have interested Madeleine at all, longed to graduate into a class genuinely competitive with her, and yet had no notion what qualities she lacked that consistently prevented her from doing so.

Till one day at the office, a friend said to her, 'Deb, if you're still looking for a flat, I've heard of something that may suit you. A friend of mine has got one she is giving up at the end of the week. I told her about you and she's agreed to give you a first refusal if you'll go round and see it this evening.'

'Where is it?' Deborah asked eagerly.

'It's just off the back of Wigmore Street,' said the girl, 'I do hope it's what you want – flats are such hell to find these days.'

After work that evening, Deborah went to see the flat and found it exactly what she wanted. There was a minute bedroom, a small sitting-room, an adequately equipped bathroom and a cupboard with a sink and cooker. The style of decoration was rather more intellectual than that of Madeleine's flat – the chairs were modern Swedish type and there were low bookcases filled with books along the walls. The rent was a guinea higher than Deborah had been paying, and the real owner, she was told, was now with the Ministry of Food in North Wales, and had no intention of coming back till the end of the war when presumably all danger of bombing would be over.

Deborah thought rapidly that while the extra guinea was a bit of a snag and would have to come out of savings, there would be a definite advantage in moving to a background she felt more typically her own; and that although there were certain advantages of social contacts to be gained by staying with Madeleine, it was rather cowardly to stay and depend on someone else for a build-up she must really make for herself. She had completely forgotten why the idea of leaving Madeleine had come into her head in the first place and arranged to move in at the beginning of the following week.

She went home to Hallam Street and decided on the threshold that she had better tell Madeleine right away. So she pushed open the door of the sitting-room and then stopped and said awkwardly, 'Oh, sorry,' as she saw that Madeleine was not alone. A man who was obviously Madeleine's Frenchman sat back in the big armchair. He was, as Madeleine had said, about forty-five, with dark hair turning grey, and a lined face with heavy eyelids. He was, Deborah realised instantly, a quite exceptionally attractive man, and in that same instant as he glanced at her and then stood up, she understood that he was greatly attracted by her.

This gave her confidence and instead of backing out of the room as she had first intended, she stood there looking questioningly at Madeleine, until Madeleine was forced to say, 'M. Pierre Décastre – Mrs Robertson.'

Deborah came into the room and sat on the arm of a chair. She said, 'Darling, I'm so sorry to break in on you like this, but I've got some news for you. I remembered the other day you said that Katherine might be coming back from India,' – she had in fact remembered it as she started speaking, – 'so when a girl at the office told me of a flat that's going, I thought I'd better have a look at it, not wanting to be left high

and dry, and so I went to see it this evening and I liked it so much I just took it then and there, and I'm moving in next Sunday.'

Madeleine was rather relieved. When she had first asked Deborah in with her she had assumed that Deborah would quickly be leading a life that approximated in standard with her own. But she had lately found Deborah's naïve priggishness rather trying, and certainly not the social asset that a woman similar to herself could have been. So she smiled and said, 'Of course, I shall be sorry to see you go, but if you really liked the place, you were definitely wise to take it.' She poured out another drink and handed it to Deborah, and asked casually, 'Just where is it?'

She saw Pierre quickly lift his eyelids and look at Deborah, and Deborah return his glance. She could have bitten her tongue out for the question as she watched Deborah, her eyes still on Pierre, give the exact address, and then quickly finish her drink and go.

IV

Deborah told Sheldon that she had to go to the country and look after her child as her housekeeper was ill. Sheldon accepted this and did not ask for her address; this annoyed Deborah who had been looking forward to withholding it, as did his omission to give her a parting present, though she had determined to be insulted by one if it had been proffered. But on her way to the country for the weekend, she convinced herself that Providence now owed her Pierre in return for

her giving up Sheldon on spec. She began to worry whether she had over-interpreted Pierre's appreciative glances and whether Providence had any alternate reward up her sleeve if she had.

At the cottage she found, to her surprise, her mother. Mrs Betts explained that she was going for a fortnight's holiday to Bournemouth and had discovered that by dropping off at Winchester she could easily get in a weekend with Deborah on her way. 'I didn't really have a chance to warn you,' she said, 'The Perivale had promised to let me know when they had a room vacant – you remember what nice people they were – and when they sent me a wire on Wednesday, I just decided to drop everything and come. But I can easily go straight on there tomorrow if you can't do with me,' she added.

Deborah was a little uncertain just how much of her mother's shrewdness she really could do with at this moment. But politeness demanded that she should press Mrs Betts to stay, and it also crossed her mind that with her immediate fortunes uncertain, there was no harm in securing her background more firmly. She asked, 'How long have you been here?'

'I'd only just taken off my coat and hat when you arrived,' said Mrs Betts, relieving Deborah's mind of the possibility that her mother had had time to be influenced by Mrs Chalmers before she had the opportunity to state her own case. Mrs Betts added, 'I was so sorry to find Timmy already shut up for the night. I wanted to tiptoe in, but Mrs Chalmers said he was such a light sleeper, I'd be sure to wake him.'

'He usen't to be,' said Deborah uncertainly, and then, noticing her mother's surprise at her ignorance, said quickly, 'I do hope we're all right for food; you must be hungry after your journey.'

'I brought a roast fowl with me,' said Mrs Betts proudly. She wanted Deborah to say how clever it was of her to find a fowl to roast, what an excellent housekeeper she must be, how well her tradesmen served and loved her, but Deborah could never afford to concede this appreciation, and her mother, knowing what was expected of her, said in pleased tones, 'How smart you look,' and then, really noticing her, 'You *do* look smart.'

Now she raked Deborah from head to foot, appraising the silk stockings, the faint smell of perfume, pricing the pigskin handbag, the ornament on the lapel. She said sharply, 'I haven't seen that hat before, have I?' and then critically, 'I thought you didn't like wearing hats in the country.' Deborah now thoroughly defensive, replied, 'It's my most useful hat, I've got to wear one for the office and I go straight from there to the station; it's easier to wear a hat than to carry one in crowded country buses.'

'Crowded isn't the word for travelling nowadays,' said Mrs Betts, and they talked of travelling and kindred subjects till dinner was over.

After dinner, Mrs Betts began. 'Well, Deborah,' she said, 'and are you liking London as you expected to?'

Deborah immediately said, 'Yes, you were absolutely right to suggest my getting a job. I can't tell you how much better I feel, having something to occupy me all day.'

'And all night too,' said Mrs Betts dispassionately, looking down at her heavy gold wedding-ring.

'What the hell do you mean?' asked Deborah, panic-stricken. Had someone talked about her, she wondered frantically, or had her mother really come through London and seen Madeleine, or —. She again had the sense of utter and terrifying desolation that had always confronted her when her mother found her out in a lie. Mrs Betts said, 'I'm not quite a fool, you know, Deborah, even if I don't live in the West End and go to night-clubs. You never got enough out of your job to buy yourself a pigskin bag at present-day prices, nor enough to make you tell me how much better you feel.'

No quick convincing lie sprang to Deborah's mind. She could only say defiantly, 'Well, even if what you think is true, it's not all that wrong. You've never had to do without your husband and in any case, you're different from me. Some women can do without a man and some can't, and I'm one of those that can't.'

This excuse, Mrs Betts, oddly enough, was prepared to accept. She herself, it was true, had never felt these strong, urges people talked and wrote about nowadays, but she had had a certain amount of trouble with Ernest when they were both young, and she had always assumed that all she found unsympathetic in Deborah was the workings of this incomprehensible urge that the girl must have inherited from her father. So she was not in a position to say, as she would have liked, that other women had these desires and managed to suppress them, since she was uncertain whether this was so, or whether, as she knew Deborah must believe, that these women who seemingly suppressed them, were perhaps the ones who never felt them. She said instead, 'I hope you haven't forgotten that you've got a husband and a baby.'

Deborah trotted out the arguments she and Joe had leaned on, the gain to her nerves, the gain of her serenity to her son. Mrs Betts said, 'I'll know how much of that to believe when I've seen Timmy. Meanwhile, what about Graham? He didn't strike me as the type to take kindly to this sort of gallivanting.'

Deborah tried to say with dignity, 'Graham and I understand each other.' Unfortunately she added, 'Anyway, I don't suppose he's living all that chaste himself.'

'If your new life,' said Mrs Betts, 'has merely taught you to be crude, I can't say I'm very much impressed by it so far.' She went with stately tread upstairs to bed, leaving Deborah to wonder angrily why her mother never seemed to find her as enchanting, sincere and protectable as, say, Joe did.

V

After seeing Timmy, Mrs Betts was even more uncertain of her attitude. She saw with distaste that Deborah simply found the child a bore to whom it was her duty to be polite, but on whom her time was really being wasted. She had thought, during the past months, that Deborah's separation from Timmy might make her value him more highly, but clearly Deborah's loves were all of the sort that withered with separation. Mrs Betts noticed with displeasure that Deborah was most pleased by the child when he came to woo her, to offer his toys in lumpy newspaper-wrapped parcels; then Deborah showed him the same courteously enthusiastic appreciation that, her mother felt, she must have offered to the man who presented the pigskin handbag. But when Timmy said plaintively that he wanted to be a good boy, Deborah immediately told him to run off to Mrs Chalmers.

But against all this, Mrs Betts had to admit that somewhat of Deborah's claims was true. She *was* more serene to Timmy, she didn't nag him or whine at him any more. And Timmy himself, however much he was feeling his mother's defection emotionally, had largely transferred his need for security to Mrs Chalmers, who was worthy of his trust. He looked well and animated and cheerful, and apart from this subservient desire to please his mother, Mrs Betts could find little to criticise. She said to herself, it might be best for that child if he hadn't got his mother coming down and upsetting him every week, and was shocked at herself for the thought.

Over supper she said to Deborah, 'Does Timmy remember his father at all?' Deborah said uncertainly that she wasn't sure and her mother said, outraged, 'Don't you ever talk to the boy about his Daddy?' But before Deborah could say she supposed she didn't, Mrs Chalmers had rushed in and offered, 'Oh, we talk about Daddy ever such a lot, Mrs Betts. You must get Timmy to show you his camel tomorrow. It's a picture of my husband on a camel in the last war,' she explained, 'but I told Timmy his Daddy would probably have been on one, so he calls it Daddy's camel now and comes to look at it every day.'

'How very nice,' said Mrs Betts smoothly, and glanced at Deborah, who was looking as sulky and jealous as she felt. I do quite often say something about Daddy to Timmy, she thought angrily, and even if I don't, that woman's got no right to drag in her blasted husband and his mangy camels. She wished desperately that she was back in London where, she said to herself, people accepted her as a charming woman and didn't spend all their time trying to make her look a fool.

But there was still Sunday to be got through and Deborah, determined that her mother should have no chance at all this time of a private talk with Mrs Chalmers, said that her boss had given her Monday morning off for moving in and so she and her mother could start off together. I can always put it right by saying that Timmy had a chill and I didn't like to leave him, she said to herself, and so efficiently did she dog her mother's footsteps that Mrs Betts had no chance of saying more to Mrs Chalmers than, 'If you *should* want me for anything, you know where to get in touch with me.' Mrs Betts didn't attempt to say anything else to Deborah about her way of life; she was altogether too disconcerted and uncertain to take any definite line, and shrank from the indecency of discussing it further when she had nothing strongly moral to say.

CHAPTER SIX

But when Deborah walked into her office that afternoon with her excuse ready, she found it was very far from all right. Apparently, her boss said, he had felt for some time that she was not really suited to the work; he felt that her undoubted talents might be better exercised in some – should he say more *human* job that would give her personality more scope. He mentioned that, as she was paid by the week, he must give her a week's notice, but if she liked to take some time off looking for something else, he would have no objection.

This came at a particularly bad time for Deborah. Just before Joe left her she had acquired some measure of self-confidence, but now this had all evaporated through a combination of happenings, the abortive misunderstood affair with Sheldon, the contemptuous disapproval of her mother, this loss of her job, and more than the others because common to them all, her sense of inferiority to Madeleine. She was constantly tormented by this, believing that none of those other things could ever have happened to Madeleine and wondering how she could possibly make herself so mature, so poised, so sophisticated that they could never again happen to her.

Walking home that evening, brooding over her miseries, she had forgotten all about Pierre, and by the time she got to the new flat, was determined to see nothing ahead of her but loneliness and disappointment. It was then with dismay, that when she climbed the four flights of stairs she saw Pierre leaning negligently against the doorpost with some flowers in his hand.

He smiled lazily at her and said, 'You see, I did not forget the address. Please may we put these in water?'

I'm all untidy, said Deborah drearily to herself, my hair's not done and I'm just in my old suit; Madeleine would never look like this, never, never, never. She looked uneasily at Pierre who was still smiling, and then remembered to look in her handbag for her key.

Pierre stepped in after her, and looked round saying, 'But how very nice this is. It suits you so much better than velvet curtains and overstuffed armchairs.'

Deborah had thought so too, when she first saw the flat. Now she was upset, believing that Pierre had realised right away that luscious sophisticated backgrounds were unsuitable to her, that she was better complemented by books on the shelves and Pipers on the walls. She said with difficult lightness, 'Oh, I'm not averse to a bit of luxury myself, but it was a case of taking what I could get.'

'I like it,' said Pierre, laying the flowers on the table and wandering to the window. He said, 'You have a view.'

'Only chimney-pots and roofs,' Deborah offered, and Pierre, his back to her said, 'Chimney-pots and roofs remind me of Paris,' and went on looking out of the window.

Deborah anxious to withdraw his attention from the unproductive impersonal, said politely, 'What good English you speak.'

Now Pierre turned from the window and said smilingly, 'And so I should. I was at school here for many years while my father was secretary at the Embassy. Also I have a good many friends here in England, so before the war I was often backwards and forwards.'

His reference to the Embassy reassured Deborah, who was uncertain of the social status of foreigners and afraid of being misled. She said with more warmth, 'I'm so sorry I haven't any drink to offer you, but I've only just moved in and I haven't made any useful contacts round here yet.'

Pierre raised his eyebrows and said with polite surprise, 'But you are coming to eat and drink with me, I hope?' Deborah said uncertainly, 'Well —' and Pierre added, 'I must warn you, we cannot go anywhere outrageously expensive because I have not got a great deal of money, and we will not go anywhere with a dance band because I like good food.' Deborah made up her mind and said, 'Well, look here, I'd love to come, but I simply must have a bath and change. I came up from the country this morning and I haven't had a chance to get really clean yet.'

'You have a lot of interesting books,' Pierre said, going over to the shelves, 'If I may choose one of them, I shall be quite happy to wait.'

'Of course,' Deborah said. She had left her possessions in the flat the previous week and so was able to take a perfumed bath, to put on the black lace underwear that Joe

had given her, her black dress, and one of her flowery veiled hats.

She came back to the sitting-room to find Pierre intently reading. She said, without bothering to notice what book it was, 'That looks absolutely fascinating, I really must read it, only nowadays I seem to get so little time for reading.'

Pierre stood up and put the book back on the shelf. 'You look even more lovely than you did when I first saw you,' he said, and took Deborah's coat from her and helped her into it.

He took her to a restaurant she had never been to before, a small comfortable restaurant with no mirrors, no chandeliers, and no obvious glitter. The waiters were courteous and the food excellent. Pierre chose a red wine for her and afterwards persuaded her to drink brandy with him. Deborah, without the usual stimulus of music and glitter, was self-consciously on her best behaviour. She listened to Pierre talking of London, of Paris, of Algeria where he had done his military training, without real attention, concerned only not to miss a cue, to show that degree of mature interest she was sure Madeleine must have shown. But the wine and the brandy unconsciously lessened her tenseness, and so when Pierre said casually, 'Why were you looking so depressed and unhappy when you came up the stairs this evening?' she answered quite naturally, 'I'd just lost my job,' forgetting that she had intended to tell a prestige-enhancing yarn about voluntarily giving it up.

Pierre said, 'That is really too bad. Have you any other possibilities in mind?'

'No, I haven't,' Deborah said, 'but I've got to find something, or I can't afford to live in London. You don't know of anything at the Free French Headquarters, I suppose? I've always heard it's rather easy to get silk stockings there.'

'No,' Pierre said gravely, 'though I have certain contacts that might provide silk stockings, if you are in need of them. But I do know of a job that might interest you. You don't happen to know something about antiques, do you?'

'A little.' No Englishwoman with pretensions to breeding will deny knowing a little about antiques.

'A friend of mine has an antique shop in the Curzon Street district,' Pierre explained, 'I believe his things are quite good; he tends to specialise in French furniture of the First Empire period. But he has some other work to do and he wants to find an assistant who would always be in the shop. If you like, I can tell him about you and you could go and see him.'

'I'd like it very much,' Deborah said, 'Is he a Frenchman too?'

'No,' said Pierre, 'he is a Spaniard, but he is in England many years now. I must remember to give you his address tomorrow.'

'Tomorrow?' said Deborah.

Pierre said, 'I rather think so,' and looked at Deborah. She shivered a little, and desired him with complete intensity: She wanted him to say, let us go now, but he ordered some more coffee and went on talking for another half-hour of Empire hangings and their application to modern décor. At last he called for his bill and they went back to Deborah's new flat.

II

Deborah got the job from the Spaniard, Julio Aradio. He proved to be a pleasant little bull of a man, noticeably foreign, but of no specifically noticeable nationality. He readily accepted Deborah as Pierre's nominee and explained the job, which seemed mostly to consist in reading a simple code of price labels and deciding how far above them each customer would be persuaded to go. The buying was all done by Julio in the intervals of complicated negotiations on mysterious business about which he was always just having to go off to see a man. When he was in the shop he was effusively pleasant to Deborah and tended to throw an arm carelessly over her shoulders, but he never made any further move towards her.

III

Deborah, lying in bed beside Pierre asked, 'Am I a good mistress?'

Pierre said courteously, 'Quite admirable,' and reached for a cigarette.

Deborah was irked by his unimpassioned answer. She pursued, 'No, but seriously, am I?'

Pierre looked at her through a haze of smoke and said, 'Seriously no.'

Now Deborah was startled. She said angrily, 'In that case, why are you here?'

Pierre said, 'But I enjoy you very much, naturally, or of course I would not be here.'

Deborah's anger died in curiosity. Here, she felt, was something that might be valuable for her to know. She asked, 'But how can you enjoy me if I'm not a good mistress?'

'You are confusing a lot of things,' said Pierre, 'I think you mean by a good mistress a woman who learns a lot of little tricks such as you read about in brown-paper-covered books. I am coming to believe that that is what most English people mean by being a good mistress, and in that sense you are not a very good mistress, thank God, as I am not looking for athletic exercise. I enjoy you because you attract me and please me, and that is nothing whatsoever to do with your knowledge of twenty positions with twenty-four variations.'

'But you said that that wasn't your idea of a good mistress,' said Deborah, puzzled because it was in fact hers, 'What do you mean by a good mistress?'

'Do you really want to know?' Pierre crushed out his cigarette and took another.

'Yes, of course I want to know.' Here, perhaps, thought Deborah, would lie that secret that Madeleine seemed so carelessly to hold.

Pierre said slowly, 'I think that being a good mistress is very much the same thing as being a good wife, only in one case the emphasis is perhaps more in the kitchen, in the other, in the bedroom. It is a question of being a temperament altogether feminine – and I do not mean by that being helpless and wearing frills. I think it is a question of wanting always to give pleasure – of being always pleased and never asking for anything a man does not already want to give you, from a diamond bracelet to an embrace.'

Deborah said, hurt, 'But I do want to please you.'

'You do want me to be pleased,' said Pierre, 'in order that I may want to go on pleasing you. But you think that your right to your pleasure comes before my right to mine.'

'Well, why not?' said Deborah. 'After all, you feel the same, and so does everyone else. It all evens out.'

'But you see,' said Pierre, 'everyone does not feel the same. Such a woman as I am speaking of finds her pleasure simply in giving pleasure to me. That is my definition of a good mistress, but it is, as I say, a matter of temperament.'

'Has Madeleine got that sort of temperament?' asked Deborah quickly, and was then angry at herself for asking, though she desperately wanted to know.

Pierre smiled at her and said, 'No, she has not. But she has sufficient experience and technique to pretend that she has, and very few men have sufficient of either to know that it is only a pretence. Besides, it is a pretence, that, as a matter of courtesy, one accepts.'

'Pierre,' said Deborah urgently, 'Will you teach me to be a good mistress?'

'I tell you it is a question of temperament,' said Pierre, 'and you do not understand, because you have not got that temperament. But you have got a lot of other things, beauty and freshness and naïvety.'

To hell with naïvety, thought Deborah angrily, I'm damned if I'm going to be put off learning what I want, just because Pierre likes me naïve. She said, 'I'm asking you to teach me to be like Madeleine. That's good enough for me.'

Pierre said in genuine surprise. 'But why should you want

that? You are married, you have a home, a child, a husband who is coming back to you. The Madeleines have none of these things. One can understand that while your husband is away, you should want to amuse yourself, but you have the possibility of a real and good life before you. Why should you ask me to teach you to enjoy the second-best?'

Because it's glamorous, you fool, because it's glamorous, Deborah thought to herself. She got out of bed, slipped on a dressing-gown and sat down at the dressing-table. With her face away from Pierre, she said carelessly, 'Oh, I think it might be rather fun. Besides, if a thing's worth doing, it's worth doing well.'

'That is certainly true,' Pierre said, watching her face in the mirror, 'But if you learn well how to pass for a good mistress in the way that Madeleine does, may you not find it a little hard to go back to being a good wife?'

'Hell, why should I?' said Deborah, leaning forward accurately to put on some lipstick. 'Besides, I don't suppose my husband's been wasting his time. We might find it considerably more amusing to be able to show each other something new.'

In the face Pierre was watching there was nothing but avidity. Repelled and disgusted he said angrily, 'Very well, I will teach you exactly what you want to know. I have three more weeks here, and in that time you can learn all I know of the tricks used by poules-de-luxe, how they wear their clothes, how they walk into restaurants, how they look at you under their lashes, how they safeguard themselves against responsibility, how they please and, most important of all, how they

pretend they have themselves received an infinity of pleasure. Is that what you want to know?'

Deborah turned round and said plaintively, 'But, Pierre, you're angry. Why are you angry with me?'

Pierre said slowly, 'I am not angry, but I am sorry and disappointed for you. But we have only three weeks, so will you please come back to bed and we will start our lessons.'

IV

Deborah wrote to Graham,

> Darling, I simply loathe bothering you, but would it be possible for you to let me have a little more money? Even though my new job pays a bit better than my last (I get commission, for one thing) the price of every-thing has gone up so much that I find it practically impossible to make both ends meet. Also, I'm in rather desperate need of some new clothes. As you know, I meant to make my old ones see me through the war, but now it's gone on so much longer than anyone expected, all my garments are virtually falling off me, and Timmy grows so fast he's out of everything now as soon as one's bought it. But don't worry too much if you can't manage it. I can always sell the pearls your mother gave me when we married . . .

V

Pierre was tired and miserable and bored when he met Deborah. Madeleine had been another experience like so many others he had had in so many places; Deborah had promised something fresh and simple and new. Now that he found that her dearest ambition was merely to grow like all the others, he was bored again and undertook her education simply as yet another attempt to relieve his boredom.

Deborah, faced with anything she wished to learn, was an apt pupil. She quickly assimilated all Pierre had to tell her about the clothes she should wear, the drinks she should ask for, the attitudes she should adopt and the emotions she should simulate or hide. Pierre became increasingly fascinated with this Frankenstein's monster he was creating, and excused himself by maintaining that he was merely accelerating a transformation that would otherwise have taken a little longer but must inevitably have taken place.

He said to her one day as they sat over their coffee in a restaurant, 'Deborah, how old are you?'

'Twenty-four,' said Deborah, 'I married just before the war, a week after my twenty-first birthday.'

'You surprise me,' said Pierre, 'I had thought you were at least five years older, and you are too young to regard that as an insult. But no – I am wrong. You look at least five years older now, but I remember when I first saw you, I thought immediately how very young you looked.'

'Well, I'm glad,' said Deborah gaily, 'Looking very young isn't one of my ambitions yet.'

'You are very fortunate,' Pierre said gravely, 'you are starting at twenty-four on a career that few women have sufficient experience to undertake until they are at least ten years older, which means, of course, that you have plenty of time ahead of you to make a great success of it, and time your less fortunate colleagues seldom have.'

'You can be sure,' said Deborah, 'that I shall make the very most of my time. You wait till you see me next time you get back to England.'

Pierre drained his glass of burgundy and said, 'I do not think I shall be seeing you again.'

'Now don't be morbid,' Deborah said. 'I couldn't be more against premonitions.'

Pierre laughed and said, 'You misunderstand me. I shan't see you again, because I shan't want to. I shall always be so ashamed of myself when I remember you.'

Deborah understood him. 'You're at least the third person,' she said, 'who has asked me if it mightn't be better if I went home to my chee-ild. Well, darling, that's just one of the things I've really thought out for myself and I know it's better to be happy than unhappy, and not only for me but for my baby as well. I like this sort of life, in fact, I love it, and seeing as how I'm hurting no one and doing myself quite a lot of good, I rather think I'll carry on with it. I've come to the conclusion that conventional morals were invented by a lot of unattractive bitches to make themselves feel good.'

'Still, conventional morals provide a very necessary framework for society,' Pierre said, 'personally, I would never outrage them.'

'Not openly, you mean.'

'Naturally,' agreed Pierre, 'and I advise you to remember that, if you can restrain the exhibitionist tendencies naturally induced by your attractive appearance. But what I was wondering was whether, after your taste of unconventional morality, you may not find it rather hard to settle down again with your husband. Have you considered that?'

Deborah said quickly, 'Oh, it'll work out somehow. There'll have to be adjustments on both sides. I'm not worrying about that just yet, anyway; there's plenty of time. Never trouble trouble till trouble troubles you.'

'I think you must have had an old nurse with a passion for aphorisms,' said Pierre. 'Now, if I have at last broken you of your adolescent taste for cherry-brandy, will you have an Armagnac?'

Deborah said, 'Please,' and laughed up into his eyes, so that he regretted madly that he had not met her now for the first time, that this was not their first evening of delighted discovery.

CHAPTER SEVEN

❦❦❦❦

'I am introducing you to an instructor in athletics,' said Pierre when he came to her flat on his last evening, 'who has also, as I promised you, means of access to silk stockings.'

Deborah, intrigued, still thought it proper to pout and say reproachfully, 'I did think you'd want us to spend your last evening alone together.'

'We have nothing sentimental between us that makes it desirable that we should,' Pierre said coldly, 'and I regret to find that you have forgotten my lesson on the proper modes and places for the introduction of emotionalism.' He was amused to notice that Deborah immediately looked abashed and kissed her lightly. 'Darling, you have no sense of humour about yourself at all – luckily, I think. But you are so charming, that if you wish for a last evening alone with me, I will willingly open a tin alone here with you and leave Luis Vardas to eat by himself the excellent dinner he will have ordered for us at the Ritz.'

Deborah quickly said, 'Oh, I don't see how we can do that, do you, without being rude to your friend,' and then, hopefully, 'He isn't really an instructor in athletics, is he?'

Pierre laughed kindly. 'Well, he is a Brazilian,' he said, 'he is also a diplomat and he is young, attractive and very, very rich. I used to know his father, years ago in Rio.'

One is apt to forget just how old Pierre is, thought Deborah; I suppose it's the difference in our ages that always made it so hard for me to be natural with him. It would be fun to meet someone young again. She asked, 'Is he married?'

'If he is, his wife is in Brazil and need not trouble you,' said Pierre, and Deborah laughed and said, 'Pierre, you have a mind like a cesspool, but I still think an evening alone together might have been fun,' and she put on her hat and they left the flat together for the last time.

II

Deborah was flattered rather than insulted by the appraising glance Luis Vardas cast over her simultaneously with standing up to receive them. She was sure of herself now, sure of her looks and her clothes and her abilities, and as Luis went to the bar to order their drinks she cast as calculating a look over his broad strong body as he had over hers.

'Will he do?' asked Pierre, and Deborah, still a little shocked at herself, said, 'Admirably, I think. I take it this is your parting gift?'

'And your finishing school,' said Pierre, 'since, as I told you, I have very little money and no taste for violent exercise.'

'I shall try to do you credit,' Deborah replied, and Luis came back with their drinks.

Deborah greatly enjoyed her dinner. Seated between two such attractive men, drinking champagne, fully conscious of wide admiration, was to experience the heights of bliss. What a pity, she thought dreamily, that one had to leave restaurants, parties, bars, leave gaiety and crowds for solitary pleasures that were tiring and certainly not all they were cracked up to be. Still, she thought, it's worth it all right, and it's quite fun, really. Soberly, she would never have admitted that she preferred the commitments of sexual society to its fundamentals; she knew only that she was happy here and now, and that the idea of going out into the dark and then being energetic was rather a bore.

She heard Pierre saying, 'Luis, may I ask you to see Mrs Robertson home for me? I am most ashamed, but I still have some packing to do and I have to leave very early in the morning.'

As Luis smilingly said how delighted he would be, Deborah had a moment's wild panic. What the hell am I doing, she thought, letting myself be handed from man to man like this. This Brazilian can't know anything about me, he must think I'm just a tart, I can't possibly let him come home with me tonight and take everything for granted. Then she saw Pierre standing up, kissing her hand and saying, 'Goodbye, Deborah, and good luck,' and she thought as she watched him leaving the room, damn it, I can't let Pierre down, this is his idea of being good to me, and I do owe him rather a lot.

III

Graham wrote,

> I can manage another hundred a year, I think, so long
> as I keep my present job. It should be all right, but jobs
> are apt to pack up on one suddenly, and if it does, I go
> back to being a lieutenant again with consequent
> decrease in pay. I'd rather you didn't sell those pearls
> – they were my grandmother's and the idea was that
> they should be handed down to Timmy's wife in the
> dim distant future. And talking of the son, have you
> got any new snaps of him you could let me have? He
> must have changed so much, and I feel I'm getting
> out of touch with him when I look at a picture nearly
> two years old. Darling, don't let me get out of touch
> with you. You won't change, will you?

IV

Deborah was still capable of feeling that an extra hundred
would be quite a lift. But she did not feel that an extra
hundred was at all the same thing as an extra two pounds a
week, and this, a letter from her bank manager informed
her, was how her husband had arranged for it to be paid. It's
so silly, she said to herself, practically everything one wants
to buy costs more than two pounds and it means one's always
going to be overdrawn, while if only Graham put it in as a
lump I could have drawn against it and been all right. But

why shouldn't I do that anyway, she thought, so long as I don't actually spend more than a hundred a year it comes to exactly the same thing, and so she went and bought Timmy an expensive new coat as a moral justification for further expenditure.

With this principle firmly in her mind she was able to ignore the letters she now began to receive from her bank to tell her that she was overdrawn. I can go up to a hundred pounds and still be all right, became her financial credo, and she did not yet notice the progressively increasing ratio of her overdraft to the passing months.

V

With Luis, Deborah's standard of living went steadily up. With Joe, living had been extravagant, but with Luis it was unlimited. The presents she had so laboriously justified from Joe, were heaped on her by Luis from the start; the promised silk stockings were only a drop in the ocean of jewels from Cartier, peaches in brandy from Fortnum and Mason. Luis, too, took it for granted that he should go with Deborah to buy her new clothes. To do so was not so much a payment he was making to her as one of the proper appurtenances of such an affair for which he delighted to pay. Deborah's initial distaste at buying from houses whose names had hitherto been glamour-dreams to her, under the obvious protection of a man who had so clearly been there so often before, was quickly mitigated by delight in the tangible results of such excursions. Expensively clothed, elaborately accessoried,

Deborah went with Luis among his friends and, finding among them names she had read or heard of, persuaded herself that she was socially bettered, that she was now one of this glittering, hitherto distant society. She ignored the fact that except with Luis she had no social contact with it at all; the exchanging of trite comments in lady's cloakrooms or in the more expensive hairdresser she now frequented came to represent to her a norm of social contacts with other women.

Yet still Deborah fundamentally disliked her affair with Luis. Pierre had put her into the position for which she had thought she longed, and still she found it distasteful because it was so extraordinarily difficult to find any sort of moral justification for it. Luis, like Sheldon, saw no need of any, but Deborah, despite Pierre's cynical apothegms, sometimes felt desperately that if only he would even pretend to love her, she would feel very, very much better about it.

Deborah found too that the sexual esotericism that so delighted Luis quickly came to disgust her. She even began to think lovingly of Graham – that was normal and nice, she recollected, but this sort of thing is disgusting and really quite unnecessary. She even began to wonder whether she had translated a normal sense of loss at Graham's absence into a false desire for more than he had ever given her, but she did not wonder deeply or often, for she could sooner put up with the worst of Luis than lose all else he was giving her.

And so, for the moral comfort of it, she stuck to her job. This she found both pleasing and easy. Julio Aradio had started his shop soon after Pearl Harbour when it became

clear to him that visiting Americans would be only too delighted for the opportunity to pick up some ancestral heirlooms in the Old Country. Consequently, his shop had never attempted to maintain those standards of integrity proper to older establishments, and the superficial and dubious knowledge of antiques that Deborah quickly managed to pick up passed for informed wisdom with her customers. Nor did she, in contrast with their ignorance, ever come to realise how inadequate that knowledge was. She believed herself to be an expert, and was acutely conscious of her good fortune in working among beautiful things. It did not in the least disturb her when Aradio, having sold, for instance, a pair of miniature globes as rare, and, he believed, unique, was able to produce an exactly similar pair for sale the next day; she had virtually no sense of causation, and was uninterested rather than credulous.

The shop also provided her with social contacts for those evenings when Luis was otherwise engaged. Many of her customers were anxious to give her dinner, and this Deborah was soon prepared to accept, though still on the clear if undefined understanding that other obligations awaited her at home. Sometimes, too, she would go and have a meal with Aradio and some other of the foreign friends with whom he so continually had mysterious business. She had asked him once what that business was, and he had replied darkly, 'I plot.' She gathered from the conversations that went on that he was principally interested in the restoration of the Spanish monarchy, but that most of his friends were much more sincere about it than he was.

Had it not been for an increasing distaste for Luis, Deborah would now have been well content with her life. Believing herself to be cultured, her cultural needs were satisfied by the shop. Believing herself to be witty, beautiful, entrancing, her belief was confirmed by the admiration she everywhere met. Believing herself to be highly-sexed, she was able to maintain this belief by deciding that Luis was abnormally so. But she also believed fundamentally, despite all that had gone before, that love, if not making everything quite all right, still made it morally very much better, and so, she told herself, she was starved for love.

CHAPTER EIGHT

❧❧❧❧

Then one Sunday evening, just as Deborah had come back, from Winchester, Madeleine came to see her. They had not met since Deborah had left Hallam Street, and she was instantly frightened and embarrassed, remembering how she had taken Pierre and feeling that with such a grievance outstanding, Madeleine could have nothing pleasant to say to her.

But pleasantness was exactly what Madeleine had come to diffuse. What a nice place Deborah had, she said, and how smart she looked – where did she get those shoes? – and what an exciting shade of lipstick. Deborah was disarmed, produced glasses and drinks, and sat and chatted with Madeleine as she had so often in the past, but with this difference, that there was no longer that galling sense of inferiority.

Till Madeleine, raising her glass, said, 'Well, here's to Pierre,' and then casually, 'I hope his wife is enjoying the benefits of his great experience now.'

Taken by surprise, Deborah exclaimed, 'I didn't know he was married.' Madeleine raised her eyebrows and said coldly, 'Didn't you?' and then relented and said, 'Well, I didn't

either, from anything he saw fit to tell me. But the man who introduced him to me told me that he was – apparently his wife's wildly attractive and still lives in Brittany with numerous children. I rather gathered he was off to France, and I wondered if he'd be seeing her.'

'Bit hard on him if he doesn't,' agreed Deborah, and found, to her surprise that this casual acceptance of a joint interest in Pierre did not embarrass her in the least. She thought he might have mentioned his wife to her and then wondered uneasily if he hadn't merely been applying his avowed principle of not commingling his private life and his affairs. But I did think I was something more to him than just another affair, she thought resentfully, then realised clearly that she wasn't, and longed again for love.

Madeleine was saying, 'I really came to see you, because I was wondering if you'd do something to help me.'

Deborah conscious of debt to Madeleine, said cautiously, 'If I can.'

'Well, it's like this,' said Madeleine, and interposed, 'Can I have another drink?' Deborah poured one out, and Madeleine went on, 'Well, in the dim distant past, when I was a child in Cheshire, I used to play with a little boy called Anthony Naysmith. His people had the next place to ours, plenty of money, in the Army for generations – you know the sort of thing.' 'Yes,' said Deborah, who had married Graham partly in the mistaken belief that that was the sort of thing he was. 'Well,' said Madeleine, 'Anthony's just been posted to a job at the War Office, and he doesn't know many people up here. His mother thought it might be rather nice if I took him

about a bit and gave him a good time. But the trouble is, I'm completely tied up just now.'

'His mother?' said Deborah questioningly; it was most unlike Madeleine to have contacts with people's mothers.

'Oh, she's got a house down in Surrey now and I see her occasionally when she comes to Town,' Madeleine explained rather hurriedly.

'I thought you said Cheshire,' Deborah said accusingly; some faint unease made her distrustful, but Madeleine explained readily enough, 'Oh, she loathes Anthony's wife, and as the house is Anthony's now his father is dead, she thought she'd better get out. But she loved the old place and detests being turned out of it.'

'What's his wife like?' Deborah asked, with increasing interest, and Madeleine said contemptuously, 'Oh, frightfully healthy-minded, frightfully good family, appalling clothes and utterly absorbed in hearth and home. She's shortly going to produce a fourth or fifth infant, I forget which, but disgustingly prolific, whichever it is.'

Deborah lit a cigarette and said, 'I still don't see quite what you want me to do about it.'

Madeleine said sweetly, 'Well, I wondered if you'd be an absolute angel and take him about a bit. I forgot to mention that he's a ravishingly attractive type, but, as I said, I really am rather tied up just now, and anyway, he's somehow or other never been taken with me.'

The last sentence was effective. Deborah would have had no interest in a man that Madeleine did not find attractive, but enjoyed the thought of attracting one who was not

attracted by Madeleine. So she said, 'Well, I'm not all that free myself just now, but I'd like to help you out if I possibly can.' They discussed dates and finally arranged that on the following Thursday Deborah would go round to Madeleine's flat for a drink and to meet Anthony Naysmith.

II

Deborah and Anthony Naysmith looked at each other with rising excitement. Deborah saw a tall young man, a lieutenant-colonel, with a tired sensitive face and slanting eyes that looked interestedly into hers. Anthony saw Deborah as she had always wished to be seen, lovely, young, ardent, exquisitely dressed, conveying to him the simultaneous impressions of luxury and frailty. He was entranced by her and she by him, and as they sat and drank and chatted with Madeleine, everything was tacitly settled and accepted between them.

Deborah said at last, 'I must really go. I said I'd be at the Dorchester at eight, and it's quarter to already.'

'May I walk you there?' asked Anthony. On the way they talked with disproportionate gaiety of impersonal things. Outside the Dorchester, he said, 'When can you have dinner with me?' 'Next Tuesday,' Deborah said and gave him her address, and went on to meet Luis.

Over dinner, Deborah did a little quiet bargaining with God in her mind and came to the conclusion that He wouldn't in the least mind her falling in love with Anthony if she didn't keep Luis on as well. But I needn't actually give Luis up till I'm sure, she argued, and animated with the exciting

prospect of new love she was so extraordinarily attractive to Luis that it became quite difficult to persuade him that she had really promised to go and see her old aunt the following Tuesday.

Nothing was easier than for Anthony and Deborah to believe themselves in love, for each was exactly what the other momentarily wanted. Anthony, after years of happy and unquestioning fidelity, was feeling that the emancipation and anonymity of uniform provided an admirable opportunity for investigation into those pleasures of which he had lately thought himself stinted; he was conventional and romantic, and the women he had met in the various provincial centres where he had hitherto been stationed had satisfied the demands of neither convention nor romance, whereas Deborah fitted the part like a glove. He was essentially a moral man, and to allow himself a divergence into immorality it was essential to his conscience that he should be infatuated, beglamoured, irresponsible – but not in love. Being in love, he thought conscientiously, as he entered into his affair with Deborah, was a phrase that belonged to his life with his wife; no man of the world admitted to being in love with his mistress.

Deborah had an instinctive and romantic understanding of his attitude, and played upon it with great effect. She represented herself to Anthony as a woman wholly swept away on a tide of passion for him, a passion that left her will-less and unresisting. She set out to convince Anthony that his love-making was the most wonderful thing she had ever experienced; it was unlikely, she thought, from Madeleine's

description of his wife, that this was an attitude he had ever encountered before, and so it proved. Both were shortly entirely bemused by each other, but for a long time there was no admission of love, for both were consciously acting their parts for a grand sophisticated affair and knew that mention of love must bring them down to the level of reality and possibly even of naïvety.

Deborah had, to her surprise, no trouble with Luis. As soon as he saw himself superseded, he drifted quietly away. Possibly he had also been getting a little bored, but Deborah did not care to dwell on this possibility. Instead, she thrust him further into the past, and would tell Anthony slightly mendacious stories of Luis and Pierre, which she had found pleased him enormously, both by convincing him that he had got hold of a really experienced woman and by flattering him that he was able to delight a woman who had known such competent Latins.

One of the conventions of an affair, to which Anthony relentlessly clung, was that a man should never mention his wife to his mistress. Deborah accepted this, as she had, in Madeleine, a willing source of information. It was initially agreed between Anthony and Deborah that Madeleine should not be told of their affair, and oddly enough, Madeleine never asked. The day after Deborah had met Anthony at her flat, she had telephoned Deborah to ask her what she thought of him, and to tell her how very much impressed by her Anthony was. After that she seemed more than willing to re-establish a girls-together friendship with Deborah and would tell her anything she wanted to know about Anthony's

background and life. But some instinct warned Deborah to conceal the closeness of this feminine relationship from Anthony.

There is nothing so efficacious in cementing a new friendship as conjoint abuse of the old friend who brought it about. Deborah, though she had now forgotten it, had established her acquaintance with her husband on just this basis; and now the denigration of Madeleine between her and Anthony provided the first stepping-stone between passion and love. Neither had originally expected to find any complementary mental attributes in each other. The discovery that these were there had a cataclysmic effect on the relationship. Each would discover with surprise that they actually liked the other, and each new discovery of humanity was yet another stepping-stone. When Anthony came to the flat one evening and found Deborah darning stockings, he was delighted to discover this evidence that she was human and real; though he would not have believed this himself, he was really a domestic man and was pleased when his affair, like his marriage in the past, showed signs of settling down. Meanwhile he was enjoying his holiday in night-clubs and smart restaurants, but always with the almost subconscious remembrance that this sort of thing had its limits and then one took to nice evenings at home.

Deborah began to believe that domesticity was one of the things she was hungry for. True, it was mostly over tables in restaurants that she and Anthony discovered their mutual likings for the countryside and plain English cooking and evenings at home, and, as the circumstances of war made it

impossible for their professed likings to be tried out together, they were able to grow even closer together in nostalgia. But the difference between them was that with Anthony the nostalgia was genuine, and this Deborah didn't know. Without bothering to think about it, she took it for granted that a London restaurant, so long as a Paris one was not obtainable, provided the world's most perfect setting for romance.

But love for a long time remained unexpressed between them, and the perfect affair flowed on without interruption from the prosaic demands of each other's previous life. Deborah knew from Madeleine that Anthony would period- ically go home to see his wife and family; thus, when he told her casually that he would be away for a few days, she was able to refrain from asking him where he was going and why, and, spared the discomfort of answering, Anthony grew greatly to admire Deborah's uninquisitive reticence. Deborah, on the other hand, was a little angered that Anthony never spoke to her of Timmy, whose photograph was prominent beside her bed; but she had learnt enough to keep silent about such parts of her private life as were not, in the telling, evocative of lascivious delights.

Till one weekend when Deborah was down at the cottage Mrs Chalmers said to her, 'I haven't been wanting to bother you, Mrs Robertson, but I wonder if you have been thinking when it would be convenient for me to take my holidays. Not that I'm wanting to go away from Timmy, but I don't feel it's quite fair to myself not to have a break. After all,' she ended a little belligerently, 'we all of us need a change now and again.'

Damn the woman, was Deborah's first reaction. But nowadays she seldom gave an emotion spontaneous play, so she was able to smile and say sweetly, 'Don't think I've forgotten about you, Mrs Chalmers. I've been trying to find out from my boss when it's easiest for him to let me go, but you know what it is in wartime.' Her smile changed to martyred sadness, and Mrs Chalmers, who was rather uncertain as to the nature of Deborah's work in London, wondered if she was being unpatriotic in making Mrs Robertson take time off from her important job. She said uncertainly, 'Well, I wouldn't mind putting my holiday off just a bit longer if it would make things easier for you,' but Deborah had just been visited by a brilliant idea. She said firmly, 'I wouldn't dream of it, Mrs Chalmers, you do too much for me as it is. I'll definitely fix a date with my boss and then I'll be able to let you know next weekend.'

On Monday she arranged with Aradio for a fortnight's holiday in August, in a week's time. She said nothing of this to Anthony, but showed herself to him gayer, more brilliant, more charming than he had ever known her. Then, the evening before she was due to go off, she said to him at dinner, 'I won't be able to see you for a fortnight; I've got to go to the country.'

Anthony, taken aback, forgot their customary reserve, and exclaimed spontaneously, 'Darling, why?' Deborah said gaily, 'My housekeeper is taking her annual holiday and I have to go and look after my son.' Anthony, distressed, protested, 'Darling, I can't possibly do without you for a fortnight. Can't you sneak off for a night in the middle of it?' Deborah said

firmly, 'Not possibly,' and then, 'You see, apart from the baby, I shall be quite alone in the house.' She added with a laugh, 'Why don't you invent some business near Winchester and wangle a car for it, and then you could drop in and see me.' 'Would you really like to see me if I came?' Anthony asked intently, and Deborah said, 'Don't you know that?' and sighed.

She knew already that he was having a couple of days' holiday towards the end of her fortnight, and had gathered that he had proposed going home for it. So she went quite cheerfully to the country and applied herself devotedly to Timmy, so that he should feel secure and happy and natural if a stranger should come, for she remembered with distaste his petulant behaviour during the visit of Joe.

In this she succeeded. Deborah's charm was now considerable and her son seemed no less susceptible to it than the other males she met. Deborah, eyeing him critically, thought him satisfactory. She had bought him some new sun-suits in London that showed off his straight brown limbs; his fair hair was curly with the heat and his blue eyes shone brilliantly in his tanned face. So he looked, when, on the afternoon she expected him, Anthony arrived to find Deborah and her son picnicking in the garden.

Deborah was wearing a grass-green linen frock and white pre-war sandals. She was slim and brown and lovely as she leapt up to greet Anthony and exclaimed as if overcome with pleasure and surprise, 'Oh, darling, darling Anthony, how wonderful to see you. Now everything is quite perfect.' She took him by the hand and dragged him to the rug where

Timmy sat. 'This is my son,' she said proudly, and Timmy, prepared during the past week for the great treat for the arrival of a soldier like Daddy, smiled with pleasure.

Anthony's feelings were confused. He had come down with a great burden of guilt, knowing he should be with his wife, unable to resist the pull that had dragged him to his mistress. But he had come uneasily to this admixture of two lives, this confusion of the country he so dearly loved with the furtive ecstasies he had enjoyed with Deborah.

But as he sat and took his tea and watched Deborah and Timmy he felt a great lightening of his heart. There could be no sense of anything wrong with this clean lovely girl sitting so contentedly with her baby. Nor did Deborah seek to remind him, by word or look, of all there had been between them in London. She treated him as someone dear to her, someone who had been dear to her for a very long time, and charmed both Anthony and Timmy so well that both were delighted with her.

As they went in after tea, she said casually to Anthony, 'You'll stay the night, won't you? I've got a spare room,' and she said it so naturally that Anthony was able to assume the normal demeanour of a guest and reply, 'I'd love to, if you're sure you can do with me.' 'Quite sure,' said Deborah, and smiled into his eyes. She added, 'I'll have to ask you to amuse yourself for an hour or so, while I put Timmy to bed.' Anthony said, 'I'd like to walk round the village,' and then, struck by a thought, 'But mightn't it look rather odd? I mean, you having me here while you're alone in the house?' Deborah, who had already impressed upon the village opinion the fact that

a cousin might be coming down, smiled serenely and said, 'Why should it? These people here are my friends and you are my friend too. They are nice people here,' and Anthony felt, as she had meant him to, rather ashamed and uncertain of his ground.

He came back in an hour to find Deborah in a house-coat, cooking supper. She had made up her face now and looked mature and sophisticated, but still unlike the creature of glamour and glitter he had known in London. Deborah could cook a few things well when she put her mind to it, and the meal was excellent. After dinner they sat in the garden till it grew dark and Anthony talked of foreign travel and then, inevitably, of how they must go and see those lovely places together.

As they stood up to go into the house, Anthony caught Deborah into his arms and said, 'Oh, darling, my darling, you are so sweet.' He kissed her passionately, and she let him carry her into her room and sleep with her there, murmuring, 'Oh God, you make me want you so, I can't help it, I can't help it.'

Next morning Deborah managed to wake early and creep cautiously out of bed. She sent Timmy up to call Anthony for breakfast. 'Just knock on the spare room door and shout,' she said, knowing that in the little cottage Anthony could not fail to hear. He came down to find Deborah, once again young and girlish in a cotton frock, giving Timmy his breakfast. She handed Anthony the papers, and then when Timmy had gone from the room, said, 'I didn't mean that to happen here.'

'Neither did I,' said Anthony, remembering that this house belonged to Deborah's husband, that here she was a wife and a mother. Deborah said, 'Would you understand if I asked you to go back today? And if I asked you to give me dinner on Monday after I get back?'

Anthony went, and, with no time now and no inclination to go to Cheshire, moped about London, recalling enviously the happy few hours he had spent with Deborah in the country and wishing he could be there again with her, enjoying with her now and in the future the pleasure of the country as well as the pleasures of the town.

III

Deborah had decided to retain Anthony quasi-permanently, if not to marry him. About this latter, she was not quite decided. Compared with Anthony, Graham so signally failed in every particular to achieve more than a second-best. Where Graham was socially all right, Anthony was impeccable. Where Graham was comfortably off, Anthony was rich. Where Graham was nice-looking, Anthony was outstandingly hand-some. I was very much in love with Graham when I married him, conceded Deborah, who was determined not to be one of those low girls who denied a love as soon as it was over, but there's no reason why the person who suited you at twenty should still be the right person for you at twenty-five when you've both developed and changed and in different directions too.

Still, divorce was a sordid and difficult business, and one

would have to be very very sure of Anthony before doing anything about it. If one could attach Anthony sufficiently firmly, the question of divorce could well be left for a bit. Meanwhile, Deborah argued, Anthony's the sort of person who would like to find his mistress was just as good as his wife and had a lot of other things as well.

But Deborah had not understood Anthony so well as she believed. It was true that his glimpse of her, natural and human, in the country, had made him admit to himself that he was really in love with her, but this admission was far from making him happy. The idea of marrying Deborah never even crossed his mind; for one thing, outside this affair, he was very happily married, and for another, Anthony, who was a natural snob, looked on Deborah as coming from a social class perfectly adequate for a mistress but in no way sufficient for a wife. What was worrying him was that the entry of love destroyed his freedom of action to drop the affair when convenient, and simultaneously destroyed his romantic picture of himself as the gay sensual detached lover.

None of this, however, prevented his telling Deborah next time he saw her, just how desperately he cared. They had come back to the flat now and Deborah, sensitive to some burden on Anthony's mind, answered gaily and simply, 'I love you, too, but there's nothing we can do about it.' 'No,' agreed Anthony gloomily, and then burst out, 'I wish to God it hadn't happened.' Deborah said, 'Well, it has, so let's enjoy it. Being in love is a happy thing if you make it so,' and she smiled at him and he said, 'Darling, you're wonderful,' and kissed her in passionate anguish.

The situation was too tense now to remain long at its present level, yet it was not Anthony and Deborah who relieved it, but Madeleine. Deborah, one evening when Anthony was up north, had called round at Hallam Street for a drink. She sat down and said casually, 'Well, Mady, what's the news?'

Madeleine, standing by the drink cupboard, looked round and said sardonically, 'I think it's your turn to tell me yours.'

Deborah felt a little uneasy. She said, 'Darling, what do you mean. I haven't any news to tell.'

'You don't think it might have been friendly to tell me just how well my introduction to Anthony turned out?' Madeleine said.

'Did he tell you?' asked Deborah. Something very strange was in the air, something incomprehensible and oddly frightening.

'Oh no,' mocked Madeleine, 'neither of my good friends, Anthony or Deborah, saw fit to tell me what was going on.'

'Then who did?' said Deborah, 'No one else knew.'

'Well, if you really must know,' Madeleine said triumphantly, 'I was told by Anthony's mother.'

Deborah burst out, 'How the hell did she know?'

'If you spend a large part of your time in London restaurants,' Madeleine said coldly, 'you can hardly expect people not to know sooner or later.'

Deborah said sullenly, 'I don't care if she does know, she's not going to break it up. We love each other, and it would take more than a mother to come between us.'

'How do you know she wants to?' asked Madeleine smoothly, but Deborah was pursuing her own train of thought. She went on, 'Anyway, his wife knows nothing about it.'

Madeleine said, 'She can be told.'

Now Deborah heard what Madeleine was saying. Her sense of strangeness grew. She said uncertainly, 'But no one's likely to tell her.'

'That can easily be arranged,' Madeleine said airily, 'a tactful talk with an old family friend – or perhaps a well-meant letter.'

Deborah said miserably, 'I just don't understand. I thought you were my friend. Why should you want to break it up for me? It's not doing you any harm.'

Madeleine dropped into an armchair and lit a cigarette. She said coldly, 'I think you're being just a little naïve.'

The way she said it made Deborah feel she was being a fool, that there was something here she failed to understand. She kept silent, trying to pull her thoughts together, and Madeleine went on, 'My darling Deborah, the last thing I want is to break anything up between you and Anthony.'

Deborah now remembered something that had gone before and asked suspiciously, 'Didn't I hear you say that his mother doesn't want to break it up either? Anyway, what's all this about letting his wife know? Is she going to give us her blessing too?'

Madeleine said impatiently, 'Look here, Deborah, let's cut out all the high-sounding talk and come down to brass tacks. I want to help you if you will only let me and not go on treating me as if I were your enemy. You want to keep Anthony, don't you?'

'Yes,' Deborah said, defiantly, 'I do.'

'Well, then,' said Madeleine, 'we all want the same thing. You want to get him away from his wife for your own reasons. His mother wants him to get away for hers. It's all so much easier if we put our cards on the table and work together.'

Deborah was conscious of rising distaste. She said, 'And what exactly are his mother's reasons for wanting to break up his marriage?'

Madeleine said impatiently, 'Oh, plenty. She loathes his wife – mind you, she'd loathe any woman he married – you know what these widows with only sons are like. She doesn't in the least mind him having a mistress, because that couldn't possibly conflict with her, and she could feel that she'd really got him to herself again. After all,' said Madeleine lightly, 'she comes of a generation when all men had mistresses, but never took them to meet their mothers.'

'Then she won't be any more pleased when Anthony marries me,' Deborah suggested, and Madeleine said, a little too quickly and contemptuously, 'Oh, he'd never marry you.'

Deborah suddenly saw herself as Madeleine and Anthony's mother must have seen her, as the easy woman, the professional girl-friend, the sort men had affairs with but never, ever married. Another woman might have thought now, then I'll make him marry me, just to show you, but it was not in Deborah to fight and conquer her humiliations. Rather she would run away from them, avoid them, conceal them in hatred and contempt as she now hated Madeleine and Anthony's mother and Anthony himself. She would have liked to run away now, ring up Luis, ring up any man unconnected with this shaming conception, but an unholy curiosity kept her there until she knew all there was to know. She said, as if she had not heard Madeleine's last remark, 'But I don't see why his wife should leave him just because he's having an affair. After all, she's having a baby, isn't she, and she must know that most men have affairs while their wives have babies.'

Madeleine said in a more friendly voice, 'Ah, but you don't know Rosemary. She's fiendishly jealous of him anyway and pretends to be moral and idealistic. She'd never forgive Anthony for being unfaithful to her when she was in the holy state of pregnancy, and even if she did, she'd make his life a misery with scenes and reproaches; she's not clever enough to do anything else, and that, of course, is where you come in.'

'I?' said Deborah, 'What do I do?'

'Well,' Madeleine said impatiently, 'surely you know by now there's nothing easier than to get a man when he's having a row with his wife. You tell me he's in love with you – well, then, can't you see to it that he finds scenes with his unattractive wife quite intolerable when he could be being flattered by you instead?'

'I see,' said Deborah, 'No, it shouldn't be difficult.'

'Well,' Madeleine urged, 'what about it? Shall I drop a little note to his wife?'

Deborah said slowly, 'I don't quite see what you get out of it all. I can see what his mother gets, I can see what I'm supposed to get, but I don't see where you come in.'

Madeleine looked away. She said casually, 'Oh, I'm very fond of Anthony, you know. I'd like to see him happy.'

Her manner was not quite right. 'That's not good enough,' Deborah pursued, 'You're not the sort of woman to go to all this trouble just to see that someone else is happy.'

Madeleine fidgeted a little. At last she said, 'Well, I should have thought my interest in the affair was obvious. Anthony's mother is a very rich woman – and I'm a very poor one.'

By now Deborah was expecting this answer. She thought rapidly, I might have guessed Mady would have some phoney way of making money, she can't live the way she does on what she gets; but she was not shocked. Instead she was devastated by the destruction of her romance with Anthony, for the revelation of this plot between Madeleine and Anthony's mother had, at one blow, stripped all the glamour off him. She tried to think of him as she had before, but instead, there was only the picture of a contemptible little man, pushed about like a child by two scheming women who had judged to a nicety his susceptibilities and reactions. And in this humiliation of Anthony, Deborah found herself also humiliated, for she too had been accurately and contemptuously judged.

So when Madeleine, uneasy at the tense expression on Deborah's face said, 'Well, are you going to play?' Deborah said instinctively, 'No, I couldn't possibly,' and stood up, anxious only to escape from Madeleine's knowledge of her.

Madeleine said angrily. 'I suppose your infernal priggishness is getting the better of you again.'

'Yes, it is,' said Deborah, with a burst of relief, clutching at the face-saving excuse Madeleine had tossed at her. She said, 'You may call it priggishness, but I call it decent ordinary

honesty. I'm damned if I'll have anything to do with your filthy plots.'

'You don't mind giving Anthony up?' Madeleine asked.

'You can keep him,' Deborah said, and stalked out of the room.

IV

Deborah went back to her flat and sat there shaking with humiliated fury. She said to herself, so that's what comes of being natural and falling in love with people; well, I'm damned if I'll ever be caught that way again. I tried to be decent and honest with Anthony, and all the time people were just working dirty schemes behind my back. It was still only the unfairness of being used as a catspaw that infuriated Deborah; she hated both Madeleine and Anthony's mother, because they had humiliated her and now she began to hate Anthony who had been the instrument of her humiliation. I must get rid of him, she thought, and then I can let myself go and have a good time without bothering about anyone's feelings. But to recover some of her self-respect, she would let him go only in the way that would ensure his being most unhappy after leaving her.

So when next evening Anthony called to take her to the Mirabelle, he found Deborah in a black dress and a restrained make-up ready with some cocktails. He said, 'Darling, you don't know how much I've missed you, have you missed me too?' and put his arms round her. She stood stiffly in his embrace and shut her mouth firmly as he kissed her, turning

her head away before he was ready to stop. He said uncertainly, 'Darling, what's the matter? Has anything happened?' and Deborah said emotionlessly, 'Do you mind sitting down and having a drink? I rather want to have a talk with you.'

Anthony laughed self-consciously, but obediently sat down and said, 'You've got me all worried. Suppose you put me out of my misery and tell me just what's wrong?'

Deborah said with deliberate expressionlessness, 'You didn't tell me that your wife was expecting a baby.'

Anthony recoiled, for in mentioning his wife, Deborah had broken through the convention of reticence that had always held between them. Now he said uncomfortably, 'I wasn't trying to keep it a secret. I just didn't see that it had any relevance to the situation.'

'Well, it has,' said Deborah, 'it seems to me to be quite extraordinarily relevant.'

'I really don't see,' said Anthony, 'what my wife's having a baby is to do with you and me. I didn't mention it, I admit, but frankly, it would have seemed to me in rather question-able taste to do so. Incidentally, I'd be interested to know who saw fit to tell you about it?'

'Madeleine just mentioned it casually,' Deborah said. 'Naturally she didn't know I'd have any particular interest in knowing about it.'

'And I still don't see why you have,' said Anthony, anger beginning to rise in his voice.

Deborah stared at the light till her eyes were bright with tears. She let her voice break as she said, 'You see, I've had a child myself. If I hadn't, perhaps I'd feel differently about it

all, but as it is, there's something – I suppose you might call it loyalty – that stops one woman from doing the dirty on another in those circumstances.'

Anthony said, 'Oh, my God,' and looked glumly at the floor. Deborah had, as she had intended, put him into a position where argument was impossible.

She flung herself on to the carpet at his feet, clasped his knees, looked tearfully into his face. She cried, 'Oh darling, I love you so much, it's absolute agony to me to say this to you, but I must. I can't bear to think how terrible it would have been for me if I'd discovered my husband was in love with another woman when I was expecting Timmy, and I just can't do it to her now I know.'

Anthony caught Deborah to him and groaned, 'Oh darling, you're so sweet and wonderful, I can't let you go.' He buried his mouth in her hair and wept, and Deborah sobbed at him, 'It's hell, it's unalterable hell, but we can't take our happiness at someone else's expense. I think I'll always love you and I know I'll never forget you, but I can't be a swine to a woman who's going to have a baby, somehow I just can't.'

For a few more minutes they sobbed in each other's embrace. Then Anthony gently pushed Deborah away from him. He said, 'I know what you're saying is true. I've had it on my conscience for some time, but you're so adorable I was too weak to do anything about it. But I'll never forget how wonderful you've been about all this and some part of me will always be loving you.'

Deborah's heart leapt and she thought jubilantly, he'll always be comparing his wife with me, and she won't come out

of it that well. She said in a calm and resigned voice, 'You'll not forget you were going to take me to Dubrovnik after the war,' and then buried her face in the sofa cushions again and sobbed wildly. Between her sobs she gasped, 'Please go now, go quickly, or I just can't stand it.' Anthony hesitated a moment, bent down and lightly kissed her dishevelled golden hair, then picked up his cap and stick, and left.

As soon as the door closed behind him, Deborah got up and tidied the cushions. She poured herself out another drink and lit a cigarette. That really passed off very well, she thought complacently, but that's my last dabble in emotion. Now she had an evening to waste and nothing arranged. I'd better write to Graham, she thought, and sat down to compose a charming letter full of anecdotes about Timmy and details of village life and assurances of her unchanging love.

CHAPTER NINE

❦❦❦❦❦

Now, having convinced Anthony of her magnanimity and essential goodness, it was a small matter for Deborah to convince herself of the same. So she was displeased to find Madeleine waiting for her at the flat the next evening, since Madeleine's knowledge necessitated her recalling that there was, in fact, another way of looking at the story.

But Madeleine, it soon appeared, was as concerned to put a new face on it as Deborah herself. Of course, she explained with a hurried smile, the set-up hadn't been nearly so melodramatic as she had led Deborah to believe the previous day. There hadn't been, she assured Deborah anything at all like a *plot* – she was sure Deborah hadn't really thought there was – just a casual remark by Anthony's mother one day, she was sure he wasn't really happy with Rosemary, how much she'd like to see him happy, perhaps, after so many years – well, Deborah could see how it all came about. But Madeleine hadn't really the faintest notion of anything *serious* happening when she had introduced Anthony to Deborah.

And nothing serious had, said Deborah with a contemptuous little laugh. She was afraid, she said, she'd misled Madeleine as much as Madeleine had misled her, but the

trouble was, she could never resist a really dramatic situation. 'Neither can I,' said Madeleine thankfully, and they both laughed in wary relief. 'To tell you the truth, I was getting just a little fed up with it,' Deborah added. 'Romance is very thrilling and all that, but there are limits.' 'Yes, I always think romance is rather *jeune fille*,' Madeleine agreed, and went on, 'but what I really came to ask you is whether you'd care to come round tomorrow about seven. I'm having a party, and there'll be a few really nice people there I'd like you to meet.'

Well, why not, thought Deborah, I'll be needing some new contacts after seeing no one but Anthony for so long, and that's the least Mady owes me. 'I'd love to come,' she said aloud, and Madeleine said, 'That'll be wonderful, see you tomorrow then,' kissed Deborah lightly, and floated off.

II

Left alone, Deborah said to herself, I really ought to think seriously about my position. There's one thing this Anthony affair has taught me, and that is that Joe was wrong and Graham was right. It's falling in love with people and getting all emotionally het-up that's being disloyal to Graham. But just sleeping with people I don't care a damn about doesn't touch anything that belongs to my life with Graham, it's merely satisfying a physical need, and that's one thing Joe was right about. I'm not being fair to Graham or to Timmy to let myself get nervy and bad-tempered through not satisfying it. She remembered Timmy sitting on the lawn with her,

and then a picture of Anthony sitting there too obtruded itself, but she thrust this away, for to think of Anthony now meant to remember humiliation. I must keep my life in two separate compartments, she told herself, my real life with Timmy, and what I'm doing to fill in time till Graham gets back.

III

The new contacts that Deborah wanted to make now seemed to spread themselves before her in endless profusion. Her life took on a new light-heartedness and gaiety, for with not only a succession but a ceaseless intermingling of new men, Deborah found it easy to maintain her resolve to enter into no emotional entanglements. And this refusal to do so seemed to bestow on her a greater attraction and charm since her apparent inviolability led men to suppose that she would leave them, too, emotionally inviolate. But the most important contact Deborah made at Madeleine's party was not with a man, but with a woman.

Sugar Harmon was, like Deborah, a blonde, but a blonde sufficiently different from Deborah to afford a striking contrast. Sugar had platinum hair, so pale that the curls that clustered round her head seemed almost as pink as her scalp. She was plump and soft and indolent, vicious and good-tempered. Her husband had made his money in wholesale clothing, and had retired to race-horse owning; now he was in a commercial job for the government in Buenos Aires, and Sugar, who had plenty of money of her own, was left with

a baby girl, a large house near Newbury, and nothing to do. So inevitably she had drifted to London, to live in the flat of a mother who had fled to the country, and to amuse herself lazily and lightly as the occasion offered.

She and Deborah were soon inseparable, for each found the other immeasurably useful. With another woman, for instance, one could go out to lunch, and there better one's acquaintance with men who happened to be lunching too. With another woman, one could go and drink in hotel lounges, and sooner or later one would run into a man with no need to make excuses for one's presence there. And with another woman and an empty evening, one could ring up a couple of male acquaintances to come and play bridge with far less self-consciousness than a solitary woman could invite a man without such a specific and respectable game to offer him.

It was Sugar who first had the idea of the children's party. 'My Pamela and your Timmy ought to meet,' she said one day, and Deborah sighed, 'Yes, but it's so difficult without a car. I feel so sorry for all these war babies, dumped in villages all over the country and never really meeting any nice children.'

'Well, can't we arrange a meeting in Town?' Sugar suggested, and Deborah, not liking to show her bomb-dread to Sugar, said, 'It's all so difficult. You know how tiny my flat is. I couldn't possibly squeeze Timmy and Mrs Chalmers in, and anyway, I've only got one bed and a small divan.'

Once Sugar had got hold of an enticing idea, she was determined to carry it through. 'I'll tell you what,' she said,

'I'd have to get Nanny to come up with Pamela, and I'm sure she'd be delighted to take Timmy on for the night. There's tons of room in my flat, and you could pick him up after breakfast. I was thinking of bringing Pamela up anyway, to get her hair cut; you can't get it done decently in the country.'

Now Deborah was forced to enter into competition, to agree that there were certain aspects of a well-bred child's life that would be coped with only in the metropolis. She added, 'Besides, I want to get a new photograph of Timmy to send to his father. He's always asking for one, and it would be an awfully good opportunity.'

'We'll do it,' Sugar said firmly, and Deborah, still uncertain but not liking to draw back said, 'But what shall we do with them to amuse them? There's really nothing for children in London now.'

Sugar said, 'We'll have a party.' This was her invariable solution to any situation. 'Lots of the women we know have got children, and they'd simply adore to get them all together. Anyway, I got Pamela the most divine party frock last Christmas, and she's hardly ever had a chance to wear it.'

I'd have to get Timmy something smart, thought Deborah, he's really got nothing but trousers and jerseys and I bet Sugar's brat is all dolled up. The idea of Timmy, impressive in a smart suit, admired by all her acquaintances, began to please her. If I ever bring him up to Town, she thought, he'll get all gauche and unsophisticated. I must say I like a boy who knows how to behave in a restaurant; besides, when he gets older, it's going to be so important for him. I wonder if

Aradio will give me the day off, or should I take Timmy to the shop? She was increasingly enchanted with the notion of showing off her son, and finally arranged with Sugar for a Friday about a fortnight ahead.

Conscientiously Deborah made the appointment with the photographer that was to provide the basic excuse for Timmy's visit. Therefore, she was able cheerfully to tell Mrs Chalmers of the delights ahead for Timmy and all the arrangements she had made for his well-being in London.

But Mrs Chalmers did not seem to welcome the proposed treat. She said doubtfully, 'You're sure you'll be all right with him, Mrs Robertson?'

'Naturally,' retorted Deborah, incensed. 'Do you think I don't know how to manage my own son?'

'Why, of course,' Mrs Chalmers said hurriedly, 'I was only meaning, what with a strange place and a different routine, I was wondering if he mightn't feel all put about. I suppose you wouldn't care for me to come with you, and I could take Timmy for the night to my sister in Kenton?'

Clearly this scheme was both practical and convenient, yet Deborah felt a great distaste for it. She had set her heart on Timmy's staying with Pamela's superior Nanny in the flat off Curzon Street and the advantages of a suburban house in North London paled in comparison. She said, 'Well, I'd promised my friend I'd let Timmy stay with her little girl, and I know the little girl is looking forward to having him. One does so hate to disappoint a child, but I'll tell you what: why don't you bring Timmy up on Friday morning, drop him with me, and then go on to your sister? I'm sure you'd like

the chance of seeing her, and then you could meet me and Timmy at Waterloo next day, and we could all come down together.'

Mrs Chalmers reluctantly agreed. She had been so greatly hoping that Mrs Robertson would ask her to come to the children's party too, to see Timmy in his new best suit playing with all the nice little boys and girls. Mrs Chalmers could go happily without seeing her sister for another few years, but she found it hard indeed to be parted from Timmy, and particularly hard to forego the chance of seeing his joy at such an unusual treat.

But though Deborah enjoyed the party hugely as did the other mothers there, none of the children evinced signs of rapturous pleasure. There were about ten of these of both sexes and various ages, all dressed in unnecessarily elaborate best and all slightly uneasy in the company of their mothers. The children were nearly all overtired with travelling that day to attain the party, and none of them knew each other. Most of the time, each cowered near, but not too near, their mother, who, as soon as one child showed signs of making the better acquaintance of another, broke into little cries of 'Now darling, give the little girl her toy again,' 'Now darling, don't hurt the little boy,' 'Now darling, you must wait your turn.' Only Sugar's Pamela, confident in a background she knew and the comforting presence of her own Nanny was self-confident; and self-confidence in Sugar's Pamela meant an officious pertness that made all the other mothers find pride instead of shame in the gaucheness of their own children, and whisper some remark to this effect to the men who accompanied them to the party. In no case was this man the father of the respective child.

Deborah, early in the afternoon, sought out Sugar's Nanny, whose starched superiority made her feel more socially uncertain than anyone she had met before. Nanny condescendingly praised Timmy, and, after attempting to elicit from the ignorant Deborah some necessary details of Timmy's routine, said contemptuously, 'Well, we'll manage somehow. I'm sure Timmy will be a good little man and settle down. Are you thinking of staying and kissing him good night, Mrs Robertson?'

Deborah, mindful of her fairly new Geoffrey waiting in the drawing-room, said, 'Well, to tell you the truth, Nanny, I really think it would be better if I just slipped away. If he knows I'm going, he might make a fuss about it.' Nanny, unjudging with an effort, said coldly, 'You must do just what you think best, Mrs Robertson.' And Deborah said thankfully, 'In that case, I think that's what I'll do. I'll be round for Timmy just after breakfast,' and slipped back to Geoffrey to tell him they'd be able to get away as soon after tea as he liked.

Geoffrey Holcombe, Deborah's lover for the time being, was a civil servant of great charm and selfishness. It was by the exercise of this latter faculty that he was able to be present at a tea-party on a weekday, and now he was anxious proudly to display Deborah at a sherry-party where he would meet various people who might, sooner or later, be useful to him. So it was fairly soon after tea that he said impatiently to Deborah, 'Can we slip away now?' and Deborah, glancing at Timmy momentarily absorbed in unwrapping a cracker, said, 'Yes, I really think we might,' whispered a hasty goodbye to Sugar and left the party.

It must be admitted that she did not really think of Timmy again until they had left the sherry-party and were seated in a restaurant at dinner. Then the sirens went off and simultaneously some anti-aircraft guns started firing nearby. Deborah swiftly felt for her gloves and handbag, and said, 'I must go to Timmy.'

Geoffrey had deliberately gone on talking through the siren's wail. It was conventional to ignore the noise, to flout precautions, to die in the middle of a carefully prepared epigram. The other diners in the restaurant equally were observing this convention. Only Deborah, with her tense flurry, outraged it.

So Geoffrey said in a bored voice, 'My dear, must you? The child's perfectly all right where he is, and anyway it would all be over by the time you got there.'

Deborah paused a moment, said distractedly, 'He's always so scared of the damn things, that's why I liked him being in the country where we hardly ever had them. And that Nanny didn't look a bit sympathetic. Timmy's probably in tears just now.'

While she was talking, their chicken had arrived. Geoffrey said, 'Well, anyway, sit down and eat this while it's hot, and then we can see what's going to happen. Personally, I don't think anything is. Besides, the child's probably asleep again by now, and you don't want to wake him through sheer excess of maternal solicitude.'

There was a loud explosion. Deborah said frantically. 'I *must* go,' and Geoffrey said impatiently, 'That was only a gun and you're told not to run about the streets with lumps of shrapnel falling on your head. For God's sake sit down and eat your chicken.' Deborah looked round the restaurant and saw the other diners looking at her with contemptuous curiosity. She imagined them thinking she was frightened for herself, that she was leaving in panic to look for shelter. She sat down again, and dug her nails into her palms with agony for Timmy's distress as she said calmly, 'It does seem to be dying away now. I think I *will* have my chicken and then see.' 'Thank God you're behaving like a sensible woman again,' said Geoffrey. The All Clear went before the chicken was cleared away. Deborah, relieved from her worry, became exaggeratedly gay, set herself to charming Geoffrey out of his bad temper induced by the possibility of her having superior claims to his, and took him back to the flat with her, well content.

When Deborah went to fetch Timmy next morning, she made no reference to the Alert the night before. If he'd really been upset they'd have told me, she said to herself, and I don't want to make him look a fool by asking, if he just slept through it. Nanny made no reference to the Alert, assured Deborah that Timmy had been a good little boy, and went away to pack up his bag saying that he was playing in the bedroom and she would send him in.

Pamela came in first. Deborah said, 'Hullo,' and Pamela said 'Hullo,' and put her finger into her mouth with arch naughtiness. Deborah said, 'Has Timmy been a good little

boy?' and Pamela replied, 'He cried in the night and Nanny
came to him and he wouldn't stop, but I didn't cry at all.'
Deborah hurriedly said, 'That's a pretty frock you're wearing,'
and, while Pamela preened herself, thought, it couldn't have
been because of the siren or that child would have said,
probably he just wanted his pot or something. He doesn't cry
for his pot at home, she was reminded, and she told herself,
but in a strange house and feeling lonely – and then broke
off, wishing hard that she'd never brought him to London
at all.

She heard Nanny's voice saying brightly, 'Now you just go
in and see who's there.' The door handle started twisting
and turning, and then Timmy managed the strange door and
broke in. She said lightly, 'Hullo, darling,' and he ran blindly
to her, clasping her thigh as she sat in her chair, burying his
face in her lap.

Deborah longed to take him in her arms, to hug him
frantically, but Nanny had come into the room with Timmy's
little suitcase. So Deborah unclasped his arms and said,
'Come along, fellow, we've got to be moving.'

Timmy looked round uncertainly. He said sullenly, 'Where
we going?' and then desperately, 'Where's Mo? I want Mo.'

Deborah said hurriedly, 'We're going to Mo, darling, we're
going to see her at the big station. Now say goodbye and
thank you to Nanny and Pam for looking after you and giving
you such a lovely time.'

Timmy clung to Deborah's hand. He repeated urgently, 'I
want Mo,' and tried to drag her to the door. Deborah laughed
deprecatingly and said over his head, 'I really must apologise

for my son's manners, but it's the first time he's been away from home.' Nanny said, 'I quite understand, Mrs Robertson, I've had plenty of experience with these highly-strung children. I always think in such cases the less excitement the better.' Pamela, with precocious understanding, said self-righteously, 'I didn't cry in the night, did I, Nanny?' and Deborah made over-effusive thanks and took Timmy downstairs.

In the taxi on the way to the station, she suddenly decided to stay in London that weekend. Mrs Chalmers could take Timmy back by herself, and then he could get back to his normal routine right away. He's always excited when I come down, she said to herself, and he's had enough excitement for a bit. She would not admit that she wanted above everything to avoid hearing him cry out in the night, discussing with Mrs Chalmers the reason for his cries, hearing the unspoken reproach of leaving him alone with strangers. So she handed him over at Waterloo, watched with a pang his frank relief at the comforting familiarity of Mrs Chalmers, made a hurried explanation of her need to work after so much time off, and went to a call-box to phone Geoffrey, saying to herself, thank God that's over.

CHAPTER TEN

✺✺✺✺✺

Geoffrey was succeeded by Martin and Martin by Nils from the Norwegian Navy. Usually Deborah managed to avoid any awkward interregnum between men by building one up before the last had faded away, but sometimes this would fail and a gap would yawn. Then Deborah would give a party.

Parties were a never-failing expedient among Deborah's friends, inevitably so, since few of those who attended did so without predatory motives. These parties never failed to be successful. For one thing, Deborah and her women friends were always glad to be able to provide such entertainment for the man of the moment, and he, in his turn, was gratified that she was able to do so. Then Deborah, like her friends, gradually perfected a party technique. If she was giving the party, nothing was simpler than to gather in a new man from her special position of hostess. Where she was a guest, her methods varied. Confident of her attraction, it was usually easy to spot the most eligible man in the room and concentrate on him a gaze of such specific and flattering desire that he was unlikely not to respond. Occasionally, uncertain which man offered the best possibility, she would flatter a clearly unimportant man or woman by attaching herself

to them, disregarding all others until she had extracted sufficient information about the other guests to know where most profitably to divert her attentions; this method served the double purpose of telling her what she needed to know, and, since she was clearly too attractive to be forced to the company of the unimportant, of giving her with those she would later wish to attract the appearance of being unpredatory and unobvious, possibly even unusual in a perfectly admirable and usual sort of way.

But Deborah's expenses mounted and continued to mount. At least I get my dinners free, she would tell herself, but she would forget that she could well afford the equivalent of the tin of baked beans that had constituted her dinner before she met Joe. Now her men friends paid for the luxuries they enjoyed with her, from champagne to orchids for her dress and even, occasionally, for the dress itself. But they did not pay for the luxuries that had become essential to Deborah's way of life if she was to attract men of the financial standing necessary to pay for those others. They did not pay for the taxis for the hurried dash to the hairdresser or for the hairdresser himself. They did not pay her laundry bill, no inconsiderable item these days. They did not pay for the drinks she must keep in her cupboard for hospitable offers, or, if they did, they usually expected to drink it themselves. 'Hey, what's this?' they would say, holding the whisky bottle to the light, 'Surely we didn't get through all this last Tuesday?' and to avoid awkward questions of this sort, Deborah found she must pay for a certain amount of drink herself. Still, she had thrust the question of financial capacity into the background, carelessly regarding Graham's new contribution as inexhaustible, and meticulous never to balance her outgoings against her income. So it was with stupefaction that she finally received the inevitable letter from her bank manager to tell her that she was more than a hundred pounds overdrawn, and that, roughly, he would be glad to know what she proposed doing about it.

Madeleine had come back to the flat with Deborah the evening she found the letter waiting for her. Deborah picked it up, read it and said, 'Oh, my God,' in agonised tones. She had been brought to regard an overdraft as one step away from the gutter and was completely panic-stricken.

Madeleine said with avid sympathy, 'What's the matter, darling? Not bad news, I hope?'

Deborah said dramatically, 'Read it,' and handed Madeleine the letter. Madeleine read it through with a puzzled frown, then looked up and asked, 'But what's the flap about, darling? I thought at least that someone was dead. Are you afraid that the bank manager's going to tell Graham, or what?'

'It's not that,' said Deborah distractedly, 'it's just that I don't see the faintest hope of paying it off, and I can't begin to see how it happened. It's not as if I'd been wildly extravagant or anything.'

'But, Deborah,' Madeleine said, with a laugh, 'an overdraft of a hundred pounds is literally nothing. I've had one infinitely larger than that ever since I can remember.'

Deborah snapped, 'Well, I haven't, and I don't intend to. Only I wish to God I could only see some way of coping with it.'

'Well,' said Madeleine, in practical tones, 'haven't you anything you could sell?'

Deborah cast a hurried mental eye over her recent acquisitions. There were the earrings from Joe – but those had a sentimental value, she couldn't possibly part with those. There was the lapel ornament, the watch, the brooches, the rings – but then what would she wear on her coat, her wrist, her frocks, her fingers? She might have considered parting with one or even two of these, but to do so would go only a small part of the way to meeting her needs. While as for selling her recently acquired furs, these were so much a part of her uniform that she did not even consider it.

'I've only got my pearls,' she said at last, 'and they're a sort of heirloom in Graham's family. He'd simply loathe it if I had to part with them.'

'In that case,' Madeleine suggested, 'why not pop them?'

'But how would I ever get them back?' Deborah groaned, her head in her hands.

Madeleine said casually, 'Do you play poker?'

Deborah looked up. 'Vaguely,' she said, 'At least, when we were first married, Graham and I used to play a sort of poker with some friends in Winchester. Why?'

'Oh, I play a lot,' Madeleine said, 'I usually reckon to make at least ten quid a week at it. Of course, occasionally I'm down, but sometimes I'm quite a bit to the good.'

Deborah was interested. 'Who do you play with?' she asked.

'Various people,' Madeleine explained. 'Quite a lot of people seem to like it nowadays and I can always find a game when I want one. Or sometimes I go to a little club I know.'

'But that's illegal,' Deborah burst out, shocked.

'So's your nail-varnish,' Madeleine retorted. 'Only poker is profit and nail-varnish is loss.'

'I'd like to try,' Deborah said slowly, 'but not,' she added, 'in a club.'

Madeleine said, 'There's certainly no need to go to a club if you recoil from the idea. Why don't you come along to my flat on Monday? I've got a few people coming in, and you could always have a try and see how you make out.'

Deborah did have a try and won five pounds, which encouraged her sufficiently to pawn the pearls and prepare to augment her income by poker. For some months she did so, though without ever accumulating enough to redeem the pearls. Then she had a run of bad luck and eventually found herself with the pearls still in pawn and a new overdraft of fifty pounds. Deborah paused and took stock of herself.

I was wrong to gamble, she admitted, I knew it was a wrong thing to do and now I'm in a mess. Playing poker is all right for people like Madeleine, who don't worry about money and overdrafts, but I'm definitely unhappy unless I'm financially straight. The question is, how to do it?

She considered writing to Graham, but could think of no way of explaining her need without too involved an explanation; also she doubted whether he could raise a hundred and fifty pounds without selling some stock, and that, to her fundamentally cautious Yorkshire mind, brought her only a step nearer the abyss. Sugar, of course, had a lot of money, but Deborah had always pretended that she had as much to dispense as Sugar, and such a friendship as theirs would

become intolerable if Deborah ever let herself fall into the position of petitioner. She never envisaged asking financial help from any of the men she knew. Women who took money from men were prostitutes, and for prostitutes there was no kind of moral allowance at all. At last she wrote to her mother.

Darling Mummy, she began, I feel so ashamed at not having written sooner, but you did always say I was to come to you if I got into a mess, and I know you'd sooner I appealed to you than anyone else. The thing is, I'm in a bit of a hole, and so I'm swallowing my pride to ask you if you'll help me to get out of it. I've always been such a fool about money – one kept reading in the papers about the cost of living going up, but Graham had always managed the Income Tax and that sort of thing, and so I spent like I always have, without properly understanding that things cost more and I'd actually got less. Anyway, the dreadful thing is I'm about a hundred quid overdrawn and I just can't see what to do. I'm desperately worried about it, and I loathe the idea of telling Graham; he's been so good to me already. So please, Mummy, will you advise me, because I'm so miserable and worried and you're the only person I've got to turn to.

II

Mrs Betts smiled grimly when she read this letter. It was by no means the first of its kind she had received from Deborah, and by now she was an adept at reading between the lines. If Deborah said she had been spending carefully, it was likely that she had been recklessly extravagant; if Deborah said that her liabilities were a hundred pounds, they were undoubtedly considerably more. Still, it was not in Mrs Betts' nature to resist such a letter, and this Deborah well understood. The principal pastime of Mrs Betts' life was the exercise of power, and this usually involved the humiliation of somebody else. Sooner or later Deborah invariably found herself in the position when it was worth enduring this humiliation to gain her ends, certain that her mother would never resist displaying her capacity at her daughter's expense.

But this time, Mrs Betts thought, the situation was more serious than it had been before. She had been worried about Deborah for a long time now, feeling strongly that she should take some action about her daughter, yet wholly uncertain what action, in this unprecedented situation, it were best to take, and unwilling to jeopardise her position of power as she would by action that was ineffective. But now Deborah had put herself into her hands, and the situation was hers to mould; or so she thought, as she sat in Leeds and looked up trains, determined that only on the spot could she attain full mastery of the situation, resolute that Deborah must once and for all give up this rackety questionable West End life and go and live responsibly and normally with her child and wait for Graham to come back. I should have said so in the first place, Mrs Betts told herself, I've known I was wrong all the time; now I'm going to take a firm stand.

She had looked out a train that should get her to London in time to fetch Deborah from her shop and thus preclude all possibility of evasive action. But this was May 1944, and the imminent invasion of France had disorganised all the timetables. Mrs Betts arrived in London at half-past six in the evening and had no alternative to going direct to Deborah's flat.

Deborah was entertaining John Langdale, a polished young man from the Foreign Office, who had now been her lover for about a week; and so far Deborah was delighted by him. His suave sophistication, his effortless conversation and his appreciation of excellent living were satisfactorily complementary to her own desires, and in listening responsively to his admirable epigrams she regained some of that confidence in her ability to cope with the esoteric learned that she had lost when a don from Balliol had dismissed her from her first job. She was, then, displeased when, as John was working up to the climax of one of his wittiest stories, the doorbell rang.

She was aghast when she answered it, to find her mother standing there. Deborah had never envisaged the possibility of her mother making a personal tour of investigation. Her thoughts flew to John, waiting, cocktail in hand, in the sitting-room, to complete his story. It was impossible that Mrs Betts should enjoy that story. It was intolerable that John should see in this Yorkshire matron Deborah's mother. The whole situation was entirely unendurable.

Mrs Betts was upset by the expression of distaste on Deborah's face. She said with uneasy belligerence, 'I meant to get here much earlier, but the trains couldn't be more difficult. I thought, in view of your letter, the best thing I could do would be to come and have a straight talk with you. I seem to have chosen an inconvenient moment.'

Deborah, much as she would have loved to, dared not send her mother away affronted, when she so badly needed her help. So she said with an effort, 'It's not a bit inconvenient, it's only that it was such a surprise seeing you. Do come in – I've got a friend here.'

'I thought you might have,' Mrs Betts said grimly, as she followed Deborah into the sitting-room.

John uncurled himself from his chair and stood up. Deborah made an awkward introduction and Mrs Betts curtly said, 'How do you do.' Mrs Betts was disconcerted by John. She did not know exactly what she expected to find, but it was certainly not this hitherto unknown type of such obvious polish and assurance. She sat down heavily in the chair he pulled forward for her, and prepared to bristle at him until he went.

But this John did not intend to do. Though Deborah would have hated to know it, he had pictured her with a mother like this, and was delighted to find his preconception accurate. Mrs Betts, her hackles lifted in the opposite armchair, represented a challenge stimulating to his charm, and he was determined, for his own amusement, that she should succumb to it.

So he talked to her sympathetically about her train and the difficulties of travelling, and Mrs Betts, finding sympathy soothing, gradually unbent and found herself telling him all the details of her journey to which Deborah, she knew, would never have been bothered to listen. Till John, leaning forward, said, 'Now I know what would do you good after that dreadful train. Deborah, surely we've got a cocktail left for your mother?' and Mrs Betts, recalled to her mission by the suggestion of joint ownership in the drinks, said sternly, 'No cocktail for me, Mr Langdale, I've never needed them yet. I suppose it would be asking for too much to hope for a cup of tea.'

Deborah, rising uneasily said, 'No, of course not,' and went to the kitchen cubbyhole, perforce leaving John to continue entertaining her mother.

She, for her part, was determined to make her own position quite clear. She said aggressively, 'I take it you're a friend of Graham, Mr Langdale?'

'Deborah's husband?' said John, smiling charmingly, 'Unfortunately not. I've only met Deborah since he went abroad.'

'He's an exceptionally nice man,' Mrs Betts said, and clamped down her mouth.

'I'm sure he is,' John agreed.

Mrs Betts began to feel she was making a fool of herself. Clearly this young man was quite impervious to moral reminders. Mrs Betts, no more than anyone else, liked to attack a position that no one was bothering to defend. So she tried another line. She nodded towards a snapshot of Timmy standing on the bookshelves and asked, 'Are you fond of children, Mr Langdale?'

'Extremely fond,' lied John, 'though the only ones I know really well are my sister's children and they're away in the country.'

'You haven't any of your own, then?' Mrs Betts pursued.

'Unfortunately not,' John said pleasantly. 'Somehow or other, I haven't managed to get married yet.'

This, in Mrs Betts's eyes, placed the whole situation in a more tolerable light. She was naturally more susceptible to young men than young women, and since John Langdale was unmarried, his actions could be construed as sowing his wild oats, which, though it in no way ameliorated Deborah's position, left John comparatively blameless. So she softened a little towards him, and John, understanding something of her thoughts, commented. 'That grandson of yours seems a remarkably sturdy little chap.'

'You just ought to see him,' said Mrs Betts, falling thankfully out of her censorious position into a more amiable one. And when Deborah came back with the tea, she found her mother enthusiastically singing Timmy's praises while John listened with every appearance of absorbed interest.

A spasm of jealousy awoke in Deborah. She resented her mother's ability to talk so easily and unselfconsciously to John, while she herself must always remember his wit, his learning, his keen criticism, and so censor every sentence before she presented it to him. So she said coldly, 'I don't know what your plans are, Mummy, but John and I *were* going out to dinner.'

John said quickly, 'There isn't any hurry about it. I hope, Mrs Betts, that when you feel a little more rested, you'll allow

me to give you dinner too. I've got a table at the Bagatelle; I'll just ring up and tell them to make it for three.'

'Oh, I don't know whether I can do that,' Mrs Betts said. 'I was thinking of having a quiet dinner and a talk with Deborah. Couldn't we have something to eat here, Deborah, and you and Mr Langdale put your dinner off till another night? I was hoping you would be able to put me up here; I've got to be back tomorrow for a charity committee.'

'I can make you up a bed on the divan,' Deborah said sulkily, 'But there isn't anything to eat in the place. We'd have to go out anyway.'

'Then do come out with me,' John begged of Mrs Betts, 'you're only condemning me to a lonely evening if you don't, and seriously, you won't get a meal anywhere now. Getting a table in London without booking it beforehand has passed into the realm of impossibilities.' Mrs Betts looked incredulous and he persisted, 'Really, it has, hasn't it, Deborah?' 'Oh yes, that's quite true,' said Deborah, wondering which would be less, intolerable, taking her mother along to the Bagatelle or dining alone with her.

John turned again to Mrs Betts. 'Do say you'll come,' he coaxed, 'Really, I should like you to.'

Mrs Betts considered. Certainly an evening with this extremely nice boy would be pleasanter than one spent with a disgruntled and thwarted Deborah. And, going out as seldom as she did, it would be nice to see a bit of life. Also, hadn't she come up to London to find out just what the position was, and wasn't this more likely to be discovered by seeing for herself than by being told a string of lies by Deborah? Besides,

if, as Mr Langdale said, it was really impossible to get a table anywhere, she'd only be cutting off her nose to spite her face by refusing. So she said, 'Well, that's really very nice of you, Mr Langdale, if you're quite sure you don't mind entertaining an old woman like me,' and they left the flat together.

III

With the help of a bottle of wine, Mrs Betts mellowed. She forgot the many things she had intended dexterously to find out, and succumbed to John's charms. Each liked the other increasingly. Mrs Betts delighted in his flattering attentions, and he enjoyed her racy comments on the restaurant and the company, while Deborah glowered in her chair. At last Mrs Betts remembered her and said kindly, 'If you young people want to dance, don't mind me. I'm perfectly happy sitting here and watching.' 'Care to dance, Deborah?' John asked, and Deborah said ungraciously, 'If you like,' and rose from the table.

She was in too bad a temper now to respond to him, and he, deliberately ignoring it as he talked gaily to her, thought how foolish she was to behave like this, what infinitely better value her mother was, and Deborah, feeling something of this, grew more bad-tempered than ever. They went back to their table, and Deborah, looking round, saw Sugar with a party of people in the corner. She said hurriedly, 'Excuse me,' and slipped over to join them.

Mrs Betts, looking after her, said confidentially to John, 'Now just who *is* that young woman?'

John explained, 'Her name's Sugar Harmon. I believe she's a great friend of your daughter's.'

'She looks a bad lot,' said Mrs Betts decisively. She added, 'I shouldn't think she's a fit friend for Deborah, Mr Langdale. Deborah's much simpler than she looks for all that show of sophistication, and she's very easily swept off her feet.'

John understood that this censure was no longer directed at him. Somehow he had become an ally and a friend of Mrs Betts. He said consolingly, 'I really don't think you've got anything to worry about. The war makes a lot of people go haywire, but you'll find they'll all settle down all right when it's over.'

'I'm sure I hope so,' said Mrs Betts, as Deborah came back to the table. She felt vaguely assured by John's superficial consolation, forgot that she had meant to find out so many things, how long he had known Deborah, how long he proposed going on knowing her, what were his post-war plans. Instead she accepted a glass of cherry-brandy and began to swop faintly smutty anecdotes about American soldiers.

IV

But next morning, Mrs Betts found herself in a very different position. Now that she had met John, liked him, enjoyed his hospitality, it was impossible for her to censure Deborah's relationship with him, and she knew of no other man in Deborah's life on whom to direct her censure. Finally she contented herself with making some cutting remarks about

Sugar Harmon, dragging from a not very reluctant Deborah the full details of her financial embarrassments, writing a cheque for the full amount, and leaving for Leeds again in great dissatisfaction, the straight talk that had been left unspoken weighing heavily on her conscience. But there was nothing I could have done about it from all those miles away, she told herself uneasily in the train, and tried to comfort herself with John's assurance that everything would go back to normal as soon as the war was over.

CHAPTER ELEVEN

John did not last long after this. Deborah could not forgive him for liking her mother instead of allying with herself against Mrs Betts, and John, for his part, found that Deborah's petulant display of ill-temper introduced too jarring a note of reality into the game he was playing with her.

The flying-bombs made little difference to Deborah, except that, possibly, the gaiety became a little more hectic. Flying-bombs, in Deborah's way of living, had their advantages. Chivalry now demanded that a woman should not be left alone in a top floor flat while the bombs flew past, so, as the alerts were soon more or less continuous, Deborah was seldom alone at night. Mrs Chalmers begged her to give up her job and come and stay in the country till it was all over, saying that for Deborah to risk her life with her husband away was unfair to Timmy. 'Supposing something happened to you,' she said, 'that poor child would be left all on his own,' but Deborah only laughed at her fears, and went back to London as usual on the Sunday evening train.

It was during the flying-bombs period that Ken Matthews rang up. Deborah and Sugar and their current men-friends were playing poker in Deborah's flat, for Deborah had taken to poker again, though rather more cautiously and profitably than before. The telephone rang and Deborah got up to answer it.

'Is that Mrs Robertson?' asked a slow, hesitant voice. Deborah had the impression of great shyness, and instinctively spoke more gently than usual. 'Yes, it's Mrs Robertson,' she said, 'Who is it speaking?'

'I'm Ken Matthews,' said the voice. 'I don't know if your husband ever mentioned my name, but he's a great friend of mine. I'm just back from Cairo, and he asked me to look you up. I've got a parcel he asked me to give you.' The voice broke off, breathless.

'I'm sure Graham's mentioned your name,' lied Deborah enthusiastically. 'How nice of you to get in touch with me.' She stopped. The next move was up to him.

'Well, look here,' said the voice, 'I was wondering how I could get the parcel to you.' Deborah resisted the temptation to tell him to take it to a post office, and waited. 'I wonder,' said the voice, 'if you could possibly meet me for lunch tomorrow?'

By now Deborah was feeling impatiently antagonistic to the voice with its shyness, its hesitancy, its obvious lack of sophistication. She said convincingly. 'I'm so sorry, I'm afraid I never really have lunches. You see, I'm working, and I don't get time to have a proper meal.'

Behind her, Sugar said loudly, 'What the hell!' Deborah covered the microphone with her hand and said, 'Hush!' The next move was again up to the voice.

'Well, look here,' said Ken Matthews, 'I suppose you wouldn't consider having dinner with me, would you?'

Deborah said, as if undecided, 'Well, I don't really see why not.' She added brightly, 'I'll tell you what, why don't you come round to my flat about half-past six and have a drink first?'

The voice noticeably retreated. It said hurriedly, 'Well, it wouldn't be easy for me to do that, I'm having to do quite a bit of work too. Would you mind coming along and meeting me, say, at half-past seven?' and it named a restaurant in Soho.

'All right,' Deborah suddenly agreed. She replaced the telephone and said melodramatically, 'Oh, my God!' 'Who the devil was it?' Sugar asked curiously, 'You don't usually have such trouble in bringing your boyfriends to heel.' 'It's some shy little friend of my husband's,' Deborah said, laughing, 'who sounds as if he could do with a spot of education; I should think it might be rather fun.' 'Haven't you got enough on your hands?' asked the current boyfriend, meaningfully, and Deborah reassured him and sat down to her poker again.

Deborah dressed carefully for her appointment with Ken Matthews. She discarded her new bulky jewels and her silver foxes, and wore instead, an old black taffeta frock with a white lace collar and the redeemed pearls round her neck. She wore no hat, and let her shining gold hair fall down to her shoulders. She looked closely at her face in the mirror. Anyone with any experience could see it's all phoney, she reflected, but it will probably pass muster with the unsophisticated boy-friend; she picked up her bag, and for the first

time for many months made her way from her flat to her dinner alone.

After her expectations, Ken Matthews was rather a surprise. He was a major, very tall, very thin, very fair, and considerably attractive in an ethereal sort of way. Deborah correctly guessed him to be a schoolmaster in peace time. She sat down beside him and set out to disarm his obvious dread of her by asking him quick eager questions about Graham. Gradually Ken relaxed, and began to talk quite naturally. Deborah gained the, to her, unattractive impression of a boyish cheerfulness, full of high-spirited living and plain thinking. She asked sufficient loving questions about Graham to disarm Ken, and then started to inveigle him into talking about himself.

'How long are you home for?' she asked.

Ken explained that he thought he was home for about three weeks, but he wasn't sure. He'd really been called back to report to the War Office about something, and he didn't know how long they'd want him. 'I have to go there every day,' he said, 'at least, it isn't really the War Office proper, but a dingy little office tucked away in a side street.' He named the street, and Deborah went on to ask him where he was staying and found, as she had expected, in a boarding house in Hampstead.

'By the way,' she said carelessly, 'I am right in thinking Graham said you were married, aren't I?'

Ken flushed with pleasure at this evidence that he had some real existence in Deborah's and Graham's common relationship. He replied, 'Well, yes, I am, but I haven't seen my wife since 1940. We'd got a small baby and another one expected, and some friends in Connecticut invited her out there, so we thought it best for her to go. Of course, the second child was born out there, and I've never even seen him.'

'How miserable for you,' Deborah said sympathetically. 'Have you got any pictures of them you could show me? I'd simply love to see them.'

Ken pulled out his wallet and with pathetic pride displayed innumerable snapshots of his family. Deborah cooed flatteringly over them, and Ken's heart could not help but warm to her. He asked, as he put his pictures away, 'Have you got a new one of your Timmy to show me? Graham and I keep each other posted with our children's progress, so I feel I know him almost as well as his father does.'

'I've got a new one in my flat,' Deborah said, 'I must show it to you sometime.' She waited, but he did not make the obvious answer, so she went on, 'I'd like to show you Timmy too.'

Now Ken said heartily, 'I'd very much like to meet him. I know Graham was hoping that I would. I've already spoken to him on the telephone, you know.'

'No,' said Deborah, surprised, 'how was that?'

'Well, you see,' Ken explained, 'apparently Graham doesn't know your London address, so he told me how to find you at your cottage. So I found out the number and rang up, and spoke to – your housekeeper, isn't it? She gave me your London phone number, but when Timmy heard it was a friend of Daddy's, I heard him insisting he should talk to me himself. So he did, but I'm afraid he wouldn't bring himself to say more than, "How's Daddy, I hope you're quite well."'

Deborah laughed caressingly and said, 'He's such a lamb. We really must arrange for you to meet him.' She drank up her coffee and said, 'I'm afraid I really ought to be going home now. I'm a working girl and I have to get up early in the morning.'

'May I walk you home?' Ken asked. Deborah said, 'I'd love you to,' and couldn't resist adding, 'I'm not really used to London streets at night. I'd feel much safer if you'd come with me.'

They walked home the longer way, down Shaftesbury Avenue and down Regent Street, and Deborah chatted to Ken about the many deprivations of wartime life. 'Which reminds me,' she said, 'I haven't opened my parcel, and I can't very well in the middle of Piccadilly Circus. Do you know what's in it?'

'I believe there are some sandals for the baby, and some Turkish Delight, and some nail-varnish for you,' Ken said. Deborah said dully, 'How sweet of Graham – only what I'd really been hoping for was a new bag. Look,' she said, and she dragged him over to a shop window. 'You see that black crocodile bag? I've been longing for one just like that, but they cost the earth now. I can't forgive myself for not getting one earlier when they were still reasonable.'

Ken was so palpably uninterested in crocodile bags that Deborah dropped the subject and led him to talk again of life in Cairo until, as they were crossing Oxford Street, the inevitable sirens wailed out. Then she clutched his arm and gasped, 'Oh God, how I loathe those things. I can't tell you how ghastly it is every night, sitting alone in my flat and waiting for the sirens to go, and then listening to the beastly things coming over.'

Cairo's picture of the flying bombs had been so terrifying that Ken clutched her arm in admiration of her gallantry. She said breathlessly, 'I do hope the All Clear's gone before we get to the flat. It's so comforting being with someone else, it makes it seem worse being alone again.'

Ken said stoutly, 'If it hasn't, I'll stay with you till it's over.' Deborah turned up to him wide admiring eyes and said in tones of heartfelt surprise, 'Why, that would be marvellous.' Ken felt a rush of tenderness for her and said gently, 'You must get pretty lonely at times, don't you?'

Deborah gave a realistic shudder and said convincingly, 'Sometimes it gets quite unendurable.' Then she gave a deliberately forced laugh and added, 'That's why I just can't tell you how lovely it is having you here. It makes me feel – oh, I don't know, all comforted and safe, somehow.'

They had crossed Oxford Street now and were in a quiet street. Ken found himself putting his arm round her and saying with a rush of emotion, 'You little darling'. Deborah stopped, and without a word put her cheek softly against his. Then she walked on determinedly, talking in a bright voice of her job.

They came to the entrance to the flats. At the foot of the stairs, Deborah laughed shakily and said, 'At least I'll be able to show you the picture of Timmy now,' and Ken, reassured, followed her up the stairs.

'You'd like some beer, I expect,' Deborah said as they came into the sitting-room. Reluctantly she had decided against

whisky. Ken said, yes, he could do with some beer, and wandered uneasily about the room till he thankfully noticed the snapshot of Timmy. 'I haven't seen this one,' he said, and picked it up and Deborah came behind him and leant against him as they looked together at the picture.

They both heard the flying bomb simultaneously, movement momentarily checked while they listened to its gathering volume as it rushed towards them. Deborah had unconcernedly listened to many louder, but now she flung herself upon Ken, whimpering, 'Hold me tight, please hold me tight, oh, it's so wonderful to have you here.' Gradually his arms tightened about her, and when the All Clear sounded, neither of them heard it.

II

Deborah woke unusually when the morning was still only a faint grey light through the somewhat inadequate curtains. She wondered sleepily why she was not still asleep, and then, rolling over to try to sleep again, discovered that the bed beside her was empty. She switched on the light and saw in the corner by the door Ken Matthews uneasily and furtively huddling on his clothes.

She said in a voice heavy with sleep, 'Darling, come back to bed. I'm getting cold without you.' Ken looked up and turned on her a look of such hatred that she instinctively pulled the bedclothes over her breasts and suddenly had a recollection of her own emotion of unhappiness in Peter Naughton's Baker Street flat. Disgust at the recollection, without in any

way connecting in her mind with the present experience, kept her momentarily silent.

Ken was dressed now. He turned to the door, then turned back and looked at her. He said explosively, as if it were forced from him, 'I hope to God I never see you again,' then went out shutting the door carefully behind him. Alone, Deborah switched off the light, said aloud with artificial carelessness, 'Well, that's that,' and nestled down on her side to try to sleep again.

But she could not. That voice that talks so urgently when one tries, still worried, to sleep, kept telling her, 'This must be put right, must be put right' and she would cry to herself, 'I must forget about it, he's too unsophisticated, too silly to matter,' and then again, as she felt rush after rush of shameful recollection, the voice would go on dinning into her ears, 'This must be put right, must be put right.'

At last, after the dawn had fully broken, she fell into uneasy intermittent sleep and woke, late for work, with a splitting headache. Desperately she dressed and made up a face that was no better than a haggard mask. There was no time for breakfast, and Deborah arrived at the shop an hour late, feeling like death.

Fortunately, Aradio was not in that day, and Deborah was able, in the flattery of her customers, to recover a considerable measure of confidence and gaiety, so that by the time she arrived at the Berkeley for her lunch date with Sugar she was able to tell the story sufficiently amusingly to laugh at it herself.

But when she arrived back at the shop, there was a parcel waiting for her. 'Where did this come from?' she asked

Grethe, the Dutch refugee, who had recently been engaged to cope with the increasing volume of work. 'Please, a boy in black uniform bring it,' Grethe replied, and Deborah questioned, 'A District Messenger?' 'I, I would not know,' Grethe said, turning out her hands helplessly, and Deborah said, 'Well, anyway let's see what it is,' and tore off the paper and string.

'Oh, but how lovely,' cried Grethe, and then, 'Do you not like it?' Deborah had picked up a card leaving the black crocodile bag untouched in its box. The card read,

I hope I interpreted your hints correctly. I have no experience of the proper payment for this sort of thing.

'Do you not like it?' Grethe repeated, and Deborah said hurriedly and unconvincingly, 'Yes, of course, it's lovely, isn't it?' Now she picked up the bag, opened it, held it against her skirt. 'It *is* lovely,' she said, with dawning pride of possession, and laid it on her desk beside the bag she had been carrying. She stuffed the wrappings into the wastepaper basket and said to Grethe, 'Look, I must go off early this evening. Do you think you can manage.' 'Of course,' Grethe said proudly, and Deborah added hurriedly, 'If Aradio comes in, tell him I had to get home for an urgent trunk-call.' Nowadays she lied as easily as she told the truth, and made no distinction between one and the other.

On her way home, Deborah told herself, I can't leave things like this, somehow or other I've got to put them right. I can't allow this man, she said, who's such a friend of Graham's, to

go back to Cairo with that sort of impression of me, and anyway, he's such a fool he'd let it out to Graham somehow if he didn't tell him on purpose. Beneath this overt fear of revelation to her husband lurked an overwhelming necessity to wipe out the shame in which the incident had enveloped her, though shame alone seldom drove Deborah to constructive action and it needed, in this case, the real dread of her husband's knowledge.

So Deborah went to the flat and dressed herself, as always for this particular type of emotional crisis, in a tweed suit without either hat or rouge. Then she took a taxi to the little street off Whitehall where Ken Matthews had told her he worked, and waited outside the entrance through which he must come out.

At last she saw him before he saw her. She clutched his arm and said desperately, 'Ken,' then dropped her hands quickly and said, 'I'm sorry. I simply must talk to you.'

She saw his face change to angry red. He looked down at her and said with an obvious attempt at lightness, 'What's the matter? Wasn't it enough?' and made to walk on. Deborah let her eyes fill with tears, and said again with a sob, 'Oh Ken!' More and more people were coming out behind him, looking curiously at the pair. Ken said roughly, 'What do you want?' and Deborah replied, 'I must talk to you.' 'There's nothing to talk about,' Ken said, but stood still facing her. Deborah said nothing, but looked at him through wet eyes, and at last he said, 'Well, we can't talk here. You'd better come along,' and strode swiftly into Whitehall and towards Westminster Bridge, Deborah walking beside him.

They came to Parliament Square without saying a word. Ken halted at the kerb, uncertain which way to go, and Deborah, who had made her plans, took the lead and crossed the road towards the river. They were walking along the Embankment now, and at last Ken said, still walking and looking straight in front of him, 'What was it you had to talk to me about?'

Deborah said, 'There were a lot of things – but I don't know that it's any good. I suppose I was wrong to come, but I was thinking of Graham . . .' Her voice broke in a sob.

Ken said automatically, 'You should have thought of him earlier, shouldn't you?' and strode on, Deborah sobbing beside him. At last he said in exasperated curiosity, 'Well, what *is* it all about? Since you've taken so much trouble to find me, you might as well say your piece.'

Deborah sobbed again and said, 'I'm trying to, but it's so difficult,' and then, on a wail, 'Anyway, I can't talk when you just keep walking along.'

Ken stopped and faced her, and said, 'Oh God, aren't you difficult.' Deborah stared into his face with as much distraught appeal as she could muster and he said, 'Oh all right, let's go and sit down somewhere. Where the hell can we go that's near?'

Deborah, appealed to, said as she had planned, 'There isn't really anywhere round here!' She looked wildly at the river as if hoping to see a pub rise from its grimy waters, and then said with an air of tired inspiration, 'I'm afraid there's only the Savoy,' and turned to look over the road. 'Come along then,' said Ken impatiently, and marched her in.

Now the conditions Deborah had worked for began to assert themselves and Ken was no longer master of the situation. Here, in the lounge of the Savoy, Deborah was far more at home than himself, and to maintain his self-confidence he needs must bow to the importunities of the waiter, order cocktails, assume unconsciously the rôle of the male escort. 'Nothing for me,' Deborah had said when the question of cocktails arose, and he said roughly, 'Of course you must have one,' and forced it on her. Now, having drunk his own, he was able to say to her without open hostility, 'What did you want to talk to me about?'

Deborah twirled the stem of her glass in her fingers. She looked down at the table and said slowly, 'I don't want you to think for a minute that it matters to me what you think of me because it doesn't.'

'Why should it?' Ken said, with uneasy lightness, piqued, nevertheless, at her statement.

'Why should it?' Deborah repeated calmly, 'In fact, since you've taken the trouble to insult me more deeply than any man has ever insulted me before, the last thing on earth I want is to be sitting here with you at this moment. But there's just one thing that happens to be more important than my pride, and that's my husband.'

Ken said insultingly, 'If you think I was going to tell Graham about last night, you've wasted your time. I'm not that kind of cad.'

'You *are* rather intolerable, aren't you?' Deborah commented quietly. She resumed, 'No, despite all you've done to me, I still didn't think you were that kind of cad. But you've made it pretty clear what you think of me, and however little that matters to me personally, I still think I owe it to Graham not to let you go back to him with that particular impression of his wife.'

Ken said stiffly, 'If I've misjudged you in any way, I apologise. The trouble is probably that I'm out of touch with western standards of behaviour.'

'Don't be priggish,' Deborah said sharply. 'You are determined to think the worst of me and you're being unfair. Are you prepared to listen to my side of the case?'

Ken was aggrieved at being accused of unfairness. 'I'm perfectly prepared to listen to anything you have to say,' he stated coldly, and then, to relieve his uneasiness, he beckoned the waiter and ordered two more cocktails.

Deborah waited till they arrived, then she began, still looking, not at Ken, but down at the table, 'You've been talking a lot of nonsense, you know. There's no difference between western standards and any other standards – at least, not so far as I'm concerned. My standards have been exactly what they were when Graham went away two years ago. I'm not asking for your pity, but in fairness to me you must try to understand what those two years have been like. They've been two years of unendurable unhappiness and loneliness. Graham was all my life, and since he's been gone, apart from Timmy, I've had nothing. I've done my best to build up a life for myself – I've taken jobs, I've been to parties, I've done everything – everything but one thing,' she corrected herself, 'to try to make myself happy. I've even managed occasionally to kid myself that I *was* happy, but I wasn't, you know,' she

said, looking candidly into his eyes. 'There was always the loneliness just underneath, waiting to eat me up if I gave it half a chance.'

'I can see it must have been hell,' Ken muttered awkwardly looking away from her eyes.

'I'm not grumbling,' Deborah said, 'it's been like that for most women, and we don't usually talk about it, because most people understand. There's something else I've got to say to you too, though it's horribly embarrassing to talk about,' She paused. 'I'm a normal healthy woman and the years without – well, without anything, haven't been easy. I don't expect you to understand that,' she added. 'It's not a thing men are expected to endure.' Ken blushed and muttered something inaudible. 'I'm not asking you what Graham's done,' Deborah said, 'I don't want to know. I just want you to know that I haven't, and that's part of the reason why last night happened. I won't deny I often wanted to, but – well, I knew I mustn't, and though it was sometimes difficult not to, I didn't do it; I was always on my guard against it. But when you came,' her voice softened, 'all my guards were down.'

'Why?' Ken asked, half angrily, half expectantly. 'Why should I have been any different from the rest?'

'You came from Graham,' Deborah said simply. 'Oh, I wish I could make you understand. When I went to have dinner with you, it wasn't like going to meet a stranger. I do go out to dinner with other men sometimes – I won't pretend I don't. But then I go – what's the word? – defensively, because there's always, well no, not always, but quite often the danger that

sooner or later I shall have to defend myself, have to explain why I don't do that sort of thing, and quite a lot of men seem to take it for granted that any woman whose husband's abroad is fair game. But when I met you, I didn't feel defensive at all because I know you really came as a friend.'

'I did,' confirmed Ken, a little uncertain now.

'Well, you see,' Deborah went on, 'I liked you and I liked our evening and it was all so gay and easy and so different from those other times. And talking to you about Graham somehow made him seem amazingly close to me and then, in a way, since that was because of you being there, I suppose I got you and Graham muddled up. I know that sounds silly,' she said apologetically, 'but what I mean is, I felt I could be natural with you and not defensive all the time like with other men. And that was such a nice comfortable feeling and I've wanted comfort so terribly badly.'

'I can see that,' Ken said solemnly.

'Well,' Deborah whispered, 'are you going to make me say it all? I wanted comfort and I turned to you for comfort and I suppose,' she spoke more softly, and awkwardly as if the words were forced from her, 'I wanted the other thing too, and because I'd forgotten for once to be defensive, it just happened. I didn't feel wicked then, because I was still think-ing, in a silly kind of way, that because you came from Graham it was all right. But I've had a horrible day.' She gulped. 'I've been wishing I was dead all day because I've been unfaithful to Graham, and I never meant to. But I did think at least that you understood how it happened, and then I got your – your *beastly* note, and I never wanted to see you again,

but I just had to, to try to make you understand, for Graham's sake, but now I've humiliated myself telling you this and it's been just no use.' She broke off and felt in her handbag for a handkerchief with which she delicately mopped her eyes. There was a short silence.

'Deborah,' Ken said at last, reaching out his hand and putting it over hers, 'Deborah, I do understand.'

Deborah swiftly looked up, wild hope breaking through her tears. 'Do you mean that?' she breathed, as if half fearful to believe. 'Do you really understand?'

'Really I do,' Ken said earnestly, 'I feel an absolute skunk. I suppose it's no use asking you to forgive me?'

Deborah smiled a watery smile. 'Of course I forgive you,' she said, 'It was as much my fault as yours, and anyway, you're still my husband's friend, aren't you, and that's the important thing.' She withdrew her hand from his and added more briskly, 'And now I must go home and open my tin of baked beans. I've been so worried all day I forgot to have anything to eat, and now I'm just beginning to realise I'm wildly hungry.'

She stood up, and Ken, perforce, stood up too, but he laid his hand on her arm and said, 'Look here, you can't go off like that. Can't we have something to eat here?'

Deborah said, as if with a little gush of spontaneity, 'Ken, you're nice.' Then she drooped and said, 'But you don't have to. You can't possibly want to see any more of me, I'd better go home,' and half turned as if to go.

Ken said pleadingly, 'But I do want to see more of you, very much indeed. If you do go now, I'll never forgive myself, and

what's more, I won't believe you've really forgiven me. Please do stay.'

'I can't refuse if you put it like that, can I?' Deborah said. Ken still stood hesitantly and Deborah, seeing that he was uncertain of himself, suggested, 'Hadn't you better go and see if they'll give you a table? I just want to go and powder my nose.' She came back to be told by Ken that they could have a table if they waited for half an hour, so they waited and drank and reinforced their mutual forgiveness and understanding.

Over dinner the rapport became even stronger. They walked home together and, as Deborah turned to say good night at the door, Ken leant over her and said hoarsely, 'Aren't you going to let me in to say good night properly?'

In the white moonlight he saw her expression change to anguished pain. She said softly, 'So that you can put your conscience right by insulting me again tomorrow morning?'

'Oh, darling,' cried Ken, 'darling, you know I understand now, you know I can't forgive myself for what I did to you. Darling, won't you give me a chance to show you how sorry I am? I want you so badly, you're so sweet.'

Deborah looked up at him and whispered, 'I want you too. I can't say no, oh God, I don't know what I'm doing.'

'I'll take care of you,' Ken assured her manfully as they went upstairs.

Their relationship lasted for the time Ken had in England, and on his last evening Deborah said, 'I've written a long letter to Graham for you to take with you.'

Ken fidgeted. He got up from the divan where they had been sitting and walked to the window. He stood looking

out with his hands in his pockets and said with his back to her, 'I'm not going back to Cairo.'

'But, darling,' exclaimed Deborah, 'where *are* you going then?'

'India,' said Ken, still looking out of the window.

'But I thought there was no question of you not going back to Cairo,' Deborah protested. 'Why this sudden change?'

Ken said, 'I applied for a transfer,' and Deborah said, 'Why did you do that?' as he turned and faced her. Then she understood why he had done so, and a sudden shock of desolation left her shattered. She wanted to burst out crying, to fling herself on the divan and weep, to find Graham beside her in the cottage, home and everything unchanged, Timmy an intimate acquaintance, a part of her mind and her body. She held herself taut against this unexpected thrust, this memory of emotions that had so long ceased to stir her and said with frigid sincerity, 'Please go – now, right away,' and Ken went.

There's no going back, Deborah's mind said to her all that night, there's no going back. The phrase hammered itself repetitiously on to her brain, a substitute for all argument or action, there's no going back. She did not want to think behind the phrase, to examine herself against that blinding memory of the lost unrecapturable past. Instead she repeated there's no going back, there's no going back, no profit in examining motives, in totting up gain, nothing but going forward to gaiety and loss and loss.

I think I'll have a party, she told herself as she lay in her bath. I owe lots of hospitality and God knows Ken wasn't a

stimulating companion; if it hadn't been for Graham, he's not a type I'd have wasted a moment on. So she gave her party and, as always, the new man appeared and then the next new man and then the next.

CHAPTER TWELVE

The celebration of victory was the most hectic point of Deborah's wartime life, its culmination and apotheosis. She started celebrating on the Monday evening and continued with party after party until it was time to go back to work on the Thursday. 'My dear, I don't think I was sober once after Churchill's speech,' she boasted to Sugar and Madeleine and they too boasted to her of their insobriety and intemperance.

That weekend when Deborah got to the cottage, Timmy greeted her with, 'Mummy, is Daddy coming home now that the war's over?' 'I suppose so, I hadn't thought about it,' Deborah answered carelessly, but now she was forced to do so and found the thought distasteful.

There was an air of disintegration in Deborah's life after VE-Day. Reality was constantly obtruding itself, and one after another began to withdraw from her circle as if awaking from a hangover. Men talked of plans far beyond the next day's dinner, the next week's dancing, plans in which Deborah had no part. Sugar's husband came home from South America and for a time his red-faced vigour infused vitality into their lives. Then he had a brief abortive affair with Deborah and retired ashamed, taking Sugar with him.

II

'It's very difficult to say this,' Mrs Chalmers insisted, 'and I was absolutely decided not to say anything to you until the war ended, but now I'll have to be asking you, Mrs Robertson, to be looking out for someone else.'

'But why, Mrs Chalmers?' burst from Deborah, who then wondered if the answer would be quite unendurable.

But it was not like that at all. 'It's my sister,' Mrs Chalmers explained, 'the one in Kenton with the arthritis. She's been holding on, thinking that her son and daughter-in-law would be coming back to look after her, but now Tom's going to the Far East and Kitty thinks she'd be happier with her own people in Cromer, and I must say I don't blame her. Pretty near crippled my sister is, and everything to be done for her; she's been nagging at me for some time to come and look after her, but I told her, you'll have to wait for the end of the war, I said.'

'Not all jobs pack up with the end of the war you know, Mrs Chalmers,' Deborah said, smiling gently. 'My husband's doesn't, for instance, and neither does mine.'

Mrs Chalmers was still uncertain of the scope of Deborah's job. She said doubtfully, 'But they'd have to release you, wouldn't they if you told them you'd got to be home to look after your little boy?'

'Oh, no,' Deborah affected a bitter laugh, 'they'd say, you've managed very well so far, Mrs Robertson, you'll just have to go on managing. No, I'm very much afraid this will mean a boarding school for poor Timmy; I don't quite see what else to do.'

Mrs Chalmers twisted like a cornered animal. Sincerity forced from her, 'Poor little darling!'

Deborah said simply, 'I know, but what can I do? What I hate so much is the prospect of Timmy having two big changes in such a short time.'

'Two?' queried Mrs Chalmers.

'You going,' said Deborah, 'and his father coming back. Several of my friends have had their husbands back recently, and quite a few of them have told me how much it upset the children. They'd all been looking forward to having Daddy home, just like Timmy does, but apparently when the father actually got there the complete upheaval in their lives was a tremendous psychological upset. I'm afraid,' she said with a little laugh, 'I'd been rather thinking it would be better for Timmy, because he'd have you here and you're always so marvellous at understanding him and giving him a real sense of security.'

'It would break his heart to be sent off to boarding school,' Mrs Chalmers said desperately. 'Poor little lamb, he's been talking about nothing but his Daddy coming home and doing little bits of weeding and dusting here and there to make everything nice for him. Just when do you expect Captain Robertson back, if I may ask?'

Deborah didn't really know. She knew that Graham had gone out to do some Intelligence job and, reading between the lines of his recent letters, had gathered that his return would depend primarily on the needs of the job. But she said, 'Well, his A-and-S group is 20, and they say the 20's will be out by Christmas. I certainly don't think it will be any longer than that. After all, he's had three years in the Middle East now.'

Mrs Chalmers said with tremendous resolution, 'Well, my sister will just have to wait a bit longer, that's all. If you really think it will be Christmas, Mrs Robertson, I'll stay and help you out. I'd never forgive myself if I was the cause of the little darling being packed off to boarding-school.'

Deborah felt an implicit criticism of herself in the last sentence, but, having gained her point, would not distress herself by examining it. Instead she forced herself to clutch Mrs Chalmers' gnarled hand and exclaim, 'I don't quite know how to thank you. It really is wonderful of you, and such a weight off my mind, knowing Timmy can go on being happy. I do hope your sister won't mind too much.'

'If she does, she'll have to get over it,' Mrs Chalmers said grimly. She thought to herself, nothing would induce her to give up the child until the father came back and she could be sure that he would be loved as he needed and deserved.

III

Deborah's landlady wrote to her from Blackpool to tell her tenant that she would be wanting her flat again. She gave Deborah a fortnight's notice and left her in great confusion of mind.

I'll never find another flat now, she thought distractedly, and it's not even worth while looking; where the hell am I going to live? and she went round to Madeleine to pour out her troubles.

'You don't think of going home?' Madeleine asked, and Deborah replied, 'Where? To the cottage? Good God, no. What would I find to do all day?'

'Whatever you found to do before you came to London, I suppose,' Madeleine suggested lazily, and Deborah said with a laugh, 'Do you know, I can't begin to imagine just what I *did* do. Anyway, whatever it was, I can't possibly go back and do it again, I'd go absolutely crackers.'

'Then why don't you move in here again?' Madeleine offered. 'I don't in the least mind turning Katherine out – her family have got a big house up in Hampstead, and they're all living there again now, so it wouldn't be any hardship to her. Mind you, I've no idea how long it will be before my own landlord wants his flat back, but his last letter said it wouldn't be until the New Year and meanwhile it would tide you over.'

'I'm really immensely grateful to you, Mady,' Deborah said earnestly, 'It's absolutely hell feeling one's got nowhere to live, and it would be rather fun to move in with you again.'

So Deborah and Madeleine lived together again and more closely than they had before. There were no longer many pretences between them, and both were frankly predatory, either separately or in concert as suited the moment best.

Deborah had considerably more time for her social life now, for soon her job at the antique shop died on her. 'It's no good going on,' Aradio said, 'There'll be a last profit while the Americans buy last-minute souvenirs to take home with them, and I can manage that by myself. After that, there will be

no future in it. During the war people would buy anything if it looked old or even if it didn't, but soon they will be more critical and by that time I should like to be doing something else. What will you do, Deborah?' he asked, 'Will you get another job?' and Deborah answered, 'No, I don't really think I will. I'm not desperate for the money, and anyway, I think I've deserved a rest.'

This deserved rest became Deborah's excuse for lying in bed in the flat each morning until there was something to get up for. Superficially her social life continued as it had before the peace, even enhanced by the renewal of such amenities as the petrol ration, and yet it was noticeably more unsatisfactory. Gradually the gay and witty temporary soldiers and civil servants she had known settled back into pre-war paths of society to be replaced in Deborah's life by middle-aged business men and occasionally willowy dilettantes. It was almost with relief that she found herself one day hailed in the street by her first employer, Michael Stanton, the Oxford don.

'I've often wondered what became of you,' he said, 'we must have a drink on this reunion. Come along,' and he led her into Hatchetts.

At first Deborah was uneasy with him. He knew her incapacity and had once despised her. But soon his obvious admiration of her made her feel on more familiar ground and she chatted with him lightly and, at last, asked him what he was doing.

'I've changed my job since you knew me,' he told her. 'Temporarily I'm at the War Office now, dealing with transfers

and releases. So if you've got anyone you want brought home or, alternatively, sent away, I might be ready to oblige, if you make it worth my while.'

Deborah laughed, then looked at him and was shocked to discover that he was serious. 'It's nothing to me,' he said, 'I hope to be out of this racket in another month or so, and meanwhile it's rather pleasant to be able to lend a hand to people who are nice to me. You are going to be nice to me, aren't you?' he urged, and Deborah said she thought he'd be rather a nice person to be nice to, and though he wasn't really, he was still a pleasant change from the middle-aged business men, while his temporary subjection to her gave her back some of the self-esteem she had lost by being dismissed from his employment.

She carefully thought over his offer. At first it had leapt to her mind that she must ask him to bring Graham back for her, since she had for so long taken it for granted that Graham's return was her most ardent desire. But now she began to think what that return must mean, the end of her life in London, the end of her gaiety, her pleasure, her luxurious standards, the re-establishment of normal domesticity, the taking up again of old and infinitely unwanted responsibilities. There was not, as Deborah now saw it, anything at all that was desirable to be looked for in Graham's return.

Michael Stanton referred to the subject again some weeks later. 'I'll be back in Oxford soon,' he warned her, 'If you want to take my offer up, you'd better take it up quickly. Shall I get your husband home for you? . . . or,' as he watched her face, 'shall I keep him away?'

Deborah was silent. She looked down at the floor and twisted her hands together. Michael Stanton commented. 'I see. It's like that is it? Well, I can't promise to bring it off, but I'll do what I can for you.'

IV

Soon after that, Michael Stanton went back to his college, and Deborah was relieved. She did not wish to see him after he had known her reaction to his offer, she did not even consciously wish that her covert request was carried out. But as the months went by and there seemed no prospect of Graham's return, she began to lose some of her tenseness about it and to take it for granted that, somehow or other, Stanton had pulled it off.

But towards the end of November she had a letter from Graham, from Italy.

I am on my way home, he wrote, doing various jobs on the way. But there seems to be absolutely no doubt that I shall be back in time to have Christmas in the cottage with you and Timmy, and, my darling, I go quite mad with delight when I think of it. As a matter of fact I hope to be back a good week beforehand, and I've had what I think is a marvellous idea. You must be quite fed up with cooking and housekeeping in your flat and the last thing I want is my coming back to make extra work for you, yet I do rather desperately want just a few days quite alone with you to love you before we go

down to the son. So what do you think of getting a room at some big hotel like the Cumberland where we could really go gay for a few days? If you think it's a good idea send me a line here and I'll fix everything up and let you know just when and where to meet me.

'The Cumberland,' said Deborah, when she read this. 'The Cumberland! Oh my God!' and she burst into hysterical laughter so that Madeleine, who was with her, asked, 'What's up?'

'Just read this,' said Deborah, still laughing bitterly, and handed her the letter, 'Going gay at the Cumberland for a real big treat – oh my God!'

'It does sound rather grim,' Madeleine said, handing back the letter and laughing too. 'Oh, my poor Deborah,' she said, and they sat together in their big armchairs, laughing and laughing, while Graham's letter fluttered to the floor between them.

'I'm going out,' Deborah said abruptly, 'I feel I've got to take some violent exercise. It's a bit of a blow, all this suddenly bursting over me.' Madeleine said, 'Well, don't be too long; remember that Jack and Billy are coming along later, and they said that they might be bringing some chaps with them.'

Deborah pulled on her fur coat and started to walk along Portland Place towards Regent's Park. It was just beginning to get dark, and a fine rain was falling. She walked swiftly, not trying to think coherently yet, only seething with rage and frustration and disappointment.

She banged into another woman who was walking slowly towards her. 'Sorry,' she said, and lifted her head, and then, 'Why, I know you, don't I? Didn't you come to the Slade just before I left? Wait a minute, it's – Mary – Mary Beltyre, isn't it?'

'I'm Mary Middleton now,' the girl said, 'and you're Deborah Robertson that used to be Deborah Betts. I hardly recognised you, you look so – so smart,' she finished helplessly and stood still, not as if she wanted to continue the conversation but as if there was no reason to walk on.

Deborah noticed this and asked, 'What's the matter? Why are you looking so appallingly depressed? You've been crying, haven't you?' and then, 'Is there anything I can do?'

The girl shook her head, the rain washing the tears down her cheeks, 'It's my husband,' she said, 'We've only been married six months and we thought it would be all right, but he's had to go to the Far East, and God knows when I'll see him again. He went this afternoon and I'm so miserable I don't know what to do. I just wish I was dead.'

Deborah put her arm through Mary Middleton's, and began to walk back towards the flat. She said as they went, 'You know, the last thing your husband would want is for you to mope and be miserable. He'd want to think of you being gay and having a good time. I'm going to take you back to the flat with me. I've been through it myself and I know just how you feel, and, what's more, I know just what you want, and that's a damn good party.'

Mary Middleton said slowly, 'That *does* sound rather nice – only I've got to be quite sure to catch a train back to the country at 9.42.'

'Well, come anyway,' urged Deborah, 'and we'll see how the evening goes.'

The two women turned and walked back to the flat together.

Persephone Books publishes forgotten fiction and
non-fiction by unjustly neglected authors. The following
titles are available: